ONLY ROGUE ACTIONS

A GALACTIC BONDS BOOK

JENNIFER ESTEP

To sign up for Jennifer's newsletter, scan the QR code or visit
https://bit.ly/41AGJvn

Rogue actions are like stormswords.
They can save your life—or end it.

—AUTHOR UNKNOWN

ONE

KYRION

"This is a bad idea."

I paced back and forth, my hands clasped behind my back. "An extremely bad idea. Awful. Horrible. Terrible."

Vesper leaned her right hip against the metal railing and gave me an amused look. "This morning, you thought training was a great idea. Wonderful. Marvelous. Terrific, even. You were the one who was all gung-ho to test our magic, connection, and skills."

"Training *was* a great idea. But this? This is not *training*." I stopped and swept my right arm out wide. "This is a gigantic bloody *maze*."

The two of us were standing on a concrete walkway that overlooked a fifty-foot vertical drop. Down below, on the ground level, a dull gray metal wall soared thirty feet into the air and formed an enormous circle that stretched from this side of the facility all the way to the other far, far in the distance. Inside the outer wall, dozens of other walls spiraled out, forming an abstract pattern that resembled an indecipherable circuit board.

All the walls were covered with dense green vines that were so tightly packed together they hid much of the metal underneath. Many of the vines boasted pink-star honeysuckle blossoms that were bigger than dinner plates, and even here on the upper level, the honeysuckles' sweet scent saturated the air like a Regal lady's overpowering perfume. My nose twitched, and I had to hold back a sneeze.

Between the walls, gray flagstones formed paths that curled, snaked, and twisted in dozens of directions. At first glance, the area looked like a pretty hedge maze at a Regal castle on Corios, my home planet. In fact, my mother's garden at Castle Caldaren had several pink-star honeysuckle bushes, although not on this grand or complex a scale.

Many of the paths opened into large circular biodomes which were covered with energy shields to control the temperatures and physical elements inside. Through the clear, shimmering shields, I spotted everything from autumn leaves to tropical flowers to snowdrifts, since those biodomes were fashioned after Temperate woods, Tropics rain forests, and Frozon moons.

And those were just the hazards I could see from this upper observational level. Far more traps and insidious tricks would be tucked away in the biodomes themselves.

"Forget what I said before," I grumbled. "It's not a maze. It's a bloody obstacle course."

Vesper nodded. "That's exactly what it is, and I, for one, am looking forward to exploring all the twists and turns."

She looked out over the maze, and the silver flecks in her dark blue eyes brightened with anticipation. Vesper Quill was an inventor and engineer, and she loved figuring out how things worked and especially how to make them better, faster, stronger, and more efficient. She was also a seer who never forgot anything she saw, heard, or experienced.

Her forehead furrowed in concentration. To Vesper, the maze-slash-obstacle course was a life-size puzzle, and she wouldn't stop studying it until she knew exactly where every path led.

I stabbed my finger at her. "No fair using your seer magic to map the maze in advance."

Vesper let out a shocked gasp and clutched a hand to her chest in mock outrage. "Would *I* do that?"

"Absolutely," I grumbled again. "You love to win just as much as I do."

Vesper smiled. "Well, I have to do *something* to keep up with the great Kyrion Caldaren, rogue Arrow, psion extraordinaire, and all-around badass."

I harrumphed, but my lips quirked up into an answering smile.

I was a psion, a broad term for seers, spelltechs, siphons, and anyone else with incredible mental abilities. In my case, those abilities included telekinesis, telepathy, and telempathy. For years, I'd used my psion power as the head of the Arrows, the elite warriors of the Imperium. I'd lived through more brutal battles than I cared to remember, but all the blood, pain, suffering, and death I'd seen, experienced, and doled out myself had been worth it, because it had all led me to Vesper.

Several months ago, Vesper had saved my life during a fight against the Techwave, a dangerous terrorist group that wanted to topple both the Imperium and the Erzton and become the main ruling force in the Archipelago Galaxy. Vesper and I had helped each other escape when the battleground had turned into a field of oozing lava, and all that danger, stress, and trauma had led to us forming a truebond, a psionic connection that let two people share thoughts, feelings, skills, and abilities.

At first, I had been horrified at our unwanted connection. A truebond might make two people much stronger, but in some ways, it also made them extremely vulnerable. If one person was injured, then their truebonded partner would often feel the psionic echo and pain of that injury. Cuts, bruises, scrapes, and burns could also physically appear on each person's body, even if only one person had actually been wounded.

And of course, the common, romantic notion was that if one person in a truebond perished, then their partner would shortly follow. Something I'd seen for myself when my mother, Desdemona, had sickened and died after Callus Holloway had taken too much of her power at once. My father, Chauncey, had been so devastated by the loss of his truebond with my mother that he'd flown into a drunken rage, forcing me to kill him in self-defense, even though I'd only been thirteen at the time.

After that, I *never* wanted to be connected to anyone, and I had fought tooth and nail against all my growing feelings, concern, and softness for Vesper. But one by one, she'd broken down the icy walls I'd built up over the last twenty-five years and wrapped the soft, velvety ribbon of her presence around my mind and especially around my heart. Now I couldn't imagine my life without her.

"Setting aside the matter of your obvious cheating, why is everything on this planet housed inside a dome?" I resumed my pacing. "What is wrong with actually being outside in the fresh air?"

"Because even though this is a Temperate planet, we're on a mountaintop, and it can snow here year-round," a third voice chimed in. "House Battis, the owners of this fine establishment, don't want their pink-star honeysuckles, blue-moon peonies, and other rare, expensive flowers to get frostbitten by a sudden cold snap, like the one we are currently experiencing."

Asterin Armas gestured at the dome that enclosed the entire facility and arced up hundreds of feet above our heads. Large panels of orange solar glass were fitted together with thick seams of black solar wiring that made the dome resemble a giant jigsaw puzzle. From the outside, the panels formed a solid wall of citrine orange, but they were clear on the inside, and snowflakes fluttered down from the dark gray clouds in the twilight sky.

Two weeks ago, Vesper and I had come to Gewitter, the capital city of Sygnustern, Asterin's home planet and the seat of power for the Erzton, seeking refuge from Callus Holloway, the Imperium ruler who had put an enormous bounty on us. As a siphon, Holloway was able to absorb and wield all types of energy, and he wanted to take the psionic power of the truebond connection between Vesper and me for himself. The greedy bastard was determined to use us as his bloody batteries, just like he'd done to my parents.

A familiar combination of anger, resentment, and bitterness speared through my chest, and my inner monster growled in response. I'd been trying to figure out a way to kill Holloway for years. Given his siphon power, he would just absorb any blaster bolts I fired, and he could always use the electrical power in nearby lights or energy shields to heal any wounds I might inflict with my stormsword. I could chop the Imperium ruler's head off his shoulders, and the siphon would probably still find some way to heal himself. Bloody unkillable siphon.

As an Arrow, I'd eliminated my fair share of enemies, but my lack of progress regarding Holloway was more frustrating by the day, especially given the enormous threat the siphon posed to Vesper. Perhaps today's training would give me some new insight about how to kill Holloway or at least help Vesper and me further strengthen our bond so that he couldn't siphon off so much as a single spark of our power when we inevitably faced him again. I didn't care so much about myself, but I would burn down the galaxy to keep Vesper safe.

Pew! Pew! Pew!

The sound of blaster fire drifted up out of the maze, and in the distance, bright red and orange bolts zinged through the air like colorful streaks of lightning. Whoops of laughter and excitement rang out, along with a smattering of applause, and the honeysuckles' scent took on an intense, burned note.

"Why plant all this greenery if you're just going to let people run around and shoot blasters in your maze?" I groused again.

Asterin shrugged. "House Battis made a fortune mining coal, lunarium, and diamonds several generations ago. They have money to burn, and this is how they do it."

I harrumphed. "You mean this is how House Battis shows the other Erzton nobles just how much money they have—by planting ridiculously expensive and fragile flowers and then letting people play war games inside their massive domed garden."

Asterin shrugged again. "Most of the Erzton Houses are like peacocks showing off their wealth, position, and power, and Lady Battis has never been shy about flaunting her many assets."

She gestured at the maze below. "The dome might be located in House Battis territory, but the agreement between all the major Erzton Houses states that the facility is neutral ground where anyone can train, even Hammers from other Houses."

Hammers were the elite warriors of the Erzton who got their name from the lunarium war hammers they wielded, and they were just as deadly as their reputation suggested.

"Is that why there are so many cameras?" Vesper pointed at the ceiling. "So the Hammers from the other Houses can record their training sessions?"

Several wires dangled from the domed ceiling, and each one held a black camera that looked like an oversize, rotund spider. Long seams of black solar wiring studded with bulbs also dangled from the ceiling, but there were far more cameras than lights hanging over the maze.

Asterin nodded. "Yes. All the Hammers from the Erzton Houses, including House Collier, train here several times a year. The technicians are always working on new tricks, traps, and biodomes, and they make the obstacles and the environments as challenging as possible."

In other words, the maze was far more dangerous than the pretty, placid garden it appeared to be. Wonderful.

I stopped pacing and eyed the closest camera, which was focused on the three of us. Two red dots on the front burned bright and steady, making the camera look even more like a spider. My lips curled back with disgust. As a Regal lord, I'd been a target of the Imperium gossipcasts for years, and I despised being filmed, even for something as helpful as training.

The cameras might ostensibly be here so that the Hammers could record and review their training, but I was betting the House Battis leaders also got a copy of the footage. A clever way to spy on your enemies and make sure you knew exactly how capable they were, along with their tactics, tendencies, strengths, and weaknesses.

All those cameras would soon be trained on Vesper and me, which filled me with unease. Asterin had assured us that we were safe on Sygnustern, and her stepfather and mother, Lord Aldrich and Lady Verona Collier, had given us their protection as the leaders of House Collier. But thanks to the Erzton gossipcasts, Callus Holloway had to know Vesper and I were on Sygnustern. I wouldn't put it past Holloway to get one of his spies in the Erzton to send him the footage of our training session so he could figure out the best way to capture and contain us.

"This is a bad idea," I grumbled again, still eyeing the cameras.

"It will be good for us to do a different kind of training," Vesper said, stepping over to me. "Stretch our horizons, make us think outside the box, and all that other fun stuff."

I gently brushed Vesper's dark brown hair back over her left shoulder, and the russet highlights in her locks shimmered in the soft golden glow cast by the overhead bulbs. Then I skimmed my fingertips along her collarbone, enjoying the warmth of her skin through her tempered-silk clothes, which automatically adjusted to her body heat, along with the surrounding environment. Vesper was wearing a dark blue jacket, a tactical shirt, and cargo pants with knee-high black boots, just like I was, and the Arrow uniform hugged her curves in all the right places.

I would much rather do some private training with you. Just like we did in the shower this morning. I think we both proved how flexible we are.

I sent the telepathic thought to Vesper, who shivered and leaned into my touch. A blush pinkened her pale cheeks, and the silver flecks in her dark blue eyes glimmered with desire. The same emotion rippled along the velvety ribbon of her in my mind, and my inner monster rumbled with satisfaction.

Look on the bright side, Vesper replied. *It's a huge maze, which means we could always find a quiet spot for your private training.*

It's a date.

The blush on her cheeks intensified, and her soft laughter rang through my mind.

Asterin snorted and rolled her silver eyes. Then she shook her head, making her long black ponytail slap against her shoulders. "I might not be able to hear your telepathic conversation, but I know *exactly* what you're talking about. The two of you are here to improve your truebond connection. *Not* to fool around in the maze. Got it?"

Vesper and I looked at each other, then shrugged in unison.

Asterin slapped her hands on her hips, wrinkling her dark gray coveralls. "You two are *impossible*," she muttered. "It's like dealing with two lovestruck teenagers. Follow me. If you can keep your hands off each other long enough."

She narrowed her eyes at us, then spun around and stalked away.

Vesper and I looked at each other again. I waggled my

eyebrows in a suggestive manner, and peals of laughter erupted from her lips. Answering chuckles rumbled out of my own throat.

Together we trailed after Asterin, still laughing as we moved deeper into the facility.

Asterin led us along the walkway, which circled the entire maze. I glanced over the railing, but I didn't see any steps leading down to the ground level.

"No stairs?" I called out.

Asterin shook her head, making her ponytail swish from side to side. "Not from the walkway directly down to the maze. House Battis takes safety very seriously, and everyone must check in at the control room before they can access the ground level. That way, the technicians know exactly who is down there, and no one is entering the area by accident."

"What about once you're in the maze itself?" Vesper asked. "How do you get out?"

"The technicians monitor everyone through the cameras, just in case there's an emergency, but in general, once you're inside the maze, you must either figure out how to reach the center or fight your way there," Asterin replied. "Or both, if you're a Hammer and it's a training exercise."

Asterin left the walkway and strode down a wide, enclosed corridor. Holoscreens embedded in the dark gray concrete walls flickered to life at our approach. Some screens contained images that chronicled the construction of the dome, along with the maze, while others showed smiling people who had to be important members of House Battis, given the large black *B* sigils that adorned their dark red uniforms.

The three of us went to the end of the corridor, veered around a corner, and stepped into a long rectangular space. Off to the right, a glass window revealed polyplastic benches squatting in front of gray metal lockers. Steam also wisped through that area, indicating that the locker room also contained shower stalls.

Off to the left, another glass window showed a well-stocked armory. Blasters, hand cannons, swords, daggers, and war hammers hung in neat rows on the wall. Next door to the armory was an infirmary with a couple of medtables and cabinets that held injectors and other medical supplies.

Asterin moved past those areas and headed toward the back, where a waist-high permaglass wall cordoned off a large space. She pushed through a gate in the clear wall, and Vesper and I followed her.

A long metal control panel that sloped down like a keyboard stood at the front of the space. Green knobs, red buttons, and black levers jutted up from the panel's surface, along with rows of colorful lights. I'd ridden on Imperium space cruisers that didn't have such sophisticated controls.

Several small holoscreens were embedded in the panel, and a row of holograms flickered in the air. Each hologram showed a warrior in the maze, along with notes about their armor, weapons, and psionic abilities. Their heart rates, oxygen levels, and other vital signs were also displayed.

Monitors mounted to a nearby wall showed warriors clutching blasters, hand cannons, and war hammers and moving through the maze. Tables were scattered around the rest of the room where folks could watch the holograms and camera feeds.

Asterin headed over to a man wearing a red uniform standing at the center of the control panel. He was several inches shorter than me, with narrow shoulders and a thin body. He had light brown hair and eyes, and the panel's flashing lights painted eerie glows on his pale skin.

"This is Jeffrey, the head technician," Asterin said. "He

oversees and controls the maze, and his job is to throw as many challenges at the Hammers as possible. In addition to fighting each other, warriors must also deal with whatever physical obstacles and simulated holographic enemies Jeffrey activates. Some of the biodomes are also challenges in and of themselves, given their extreme environments and elements."

Jeffrey gave us a distracted wave, his attention still on the holograms flickering in the air. He frowned, then leaned forward. His long, slender fingers danced over the control panel, twisting knobs, hitting buttons, and pulling levers like he was playing a complicated concerto. In response to his actions, fog rolled across the monitors, making the warriors stop.

Pew! Pew! Pew!

The muted sound of blaster fire erupted out of a monitor, and black *X*s appeared on the holograms of two warriors, indicating that they had been mock-killed. According to the info on the screen, the warriors were equipped with modified blasters that were set to stun instead of kill, although the weapons would still leave behind nasty bruises and minor burns to remind the fighters of their failures. A simple but effective training tool.

Jeffrey nodded with satisfaction, then spoke into a black microphone sticking up out of the panel. "Hammer One and Hammer Two, you're done for the evening. Please return to the nearest exit."

Static crackled out of the microphone. "Roger that," a man replied in a sour tone.

Jeffrey hit more buttons. Asterin, Vesper, and I watched while one black *X* after another appeared on the remaining holograms. A single alpha warrior was swiftly navigating through the fog and eliminating the other fighters.

"It's too bad Zane isn't here," I murmured. "He loves war games."

A smile tugged at Vesper's lips. "He messaged me earlier."

"And what did your annoying big brother say?"

Her smile widened. "Zane told me to forget about our true-bond training, mock-kill you in the maze, and claim victory for myself."

I snorted. "Of course he did."

Zane Zimmer was the current head of the Arrows and one of the best warriors in the Imperium. He also happened to be my long-standing rival and, perhaps most unfortunate of all, Vesper's brother.

Nerezza Blackwell, Vesper's mother, had abandoned her as a child, so Vesper had never known who her father was until several weeks ago when I'd figured out Wendell Zimmer—Zane's father and a Regal lord—was the man in question.

Two weeks ago, the Zimmers had come to Sygnustern, and Zane had finagled his way onto the Collier estate. At first, I'd thought Zane was there to capture us, per his mission from Callus Holloway. But Vesper being his long-lost sister meant a great deal to Zane, and he and Wendell had welcomed her into their family with open arms. So had Beatrice Zimmer, Wendell's mother and the current head of House Zimmer.

Most of the time, I wanted to punch the smug smirk off the arrogant Arrow's face, but Zane had given Vesper the one thing she'd always wanted—a family—and I would always be grateful to him for that.

Zane, Wendell, and Beatrice had left Sygnustern several days ago to return to Corios. I was still getting used to the fact that I was going to be shackled to Zane bloody Zimmer for the rest of my life, but Vesper was already quite fond of her brother, and Zane cared about her just as much, so I would be forced to keep the punching to a minimum. Pity.

Asterin moved past Jeffrey and walked over to a woman standing beside one of the tables. The woman paced back and forth, watching the holograms move as the warriors ran, crouched, ducked, and exchanged blaster fire in the maze. Every once in a while, she would nod her head in approval or wince in commiseration as one warrior after another was eliminated.

Just like Asterin, Siya Collier was quite lovely, with light brown skin and long black hair that was wound up into a high knot. She was wearing a jacket over a tactical shirt and cargo pants in the emerald green of House Collier, and a delicate gold pendant shaped like a *C* with two hammers crossed in front of it hung from a thin gold chain around her neck.

A large war hammer dangled from a slot on Siya's black leather belt. One side of the weapon was broad and flat, like a common hammerhead you would use to drive a nail into a board, but the other side was shaped like a thick spike that was perfect for slamming into an enemy's body. Both sides of the weapon were ringed with razor-sharp edges that would easily tear through flesh.

The hilt was gold, but the hammerhead itself was made of lunarium, a rare, precious, opalescent mineral that amplified psionic abilities and turned them into physical elements like fire, ice, lightning, and wind. As the head of the House Collier Hammers, Siya knew how to use her weapon with brutal, expert efficiency.

Siya never took her hazel eyes off the holograms. "Isn't it cool?" she said, an excited note creeping into her voice.

"Very cool," I agreed. "This is the most elaborate training facility I've ever seen."

Siya nodded, still watching the holograms, her gaze flicking from one warrior to another. Vesper and I shared an amused look. Right now, our friend resembled a child in a candy store, staring in delight at all the sweets on display.

"Who's training?" Asterin asked.

Siya's face darkened like a storm cloud had suddenly taken up residence over her head. "Roderick and his friends," she replied, her voice devoid of its previous cheerful enthusiasm. "And he's going to win, just like always."

A black *X* appeared on one of the two remaining holograms. That warrior's head dropped in defeat, while the other man raised his arms high in exultation. The holograms winked out, indicating that the training session was finished.

"Who's Roderick?" Vesper asked.

Siya turned toward us. "Roderick Battis, the heir to House Battis who manages the training facility. He is also a psion, a Hammer, and an excellent warrior."

"As much as that pains you to admit," Asterin murmured.

Siya scowled at Asterin, who arched an eyebrow in response. Unexpected tension rippled off them and pinched my telempathy like a pair of sharp fingers.

Siya's scowl melted away, and she patted the table like it was a beloved pet. "Kyrion is right about one thing. House Battis does have the best training toys."

Over at the control panel, Jeffrey hit another button, and a faint buzz sounded, like a gate opening. He glanced over his shoulder at Siya. "Roderick and the House Battis Hammers are leaving the maze. Your group can get ready to enter now, Lady Siya."

Siya nodded at him and stepped away from the table. Vesper, Asterin, and I followed the Erzton lady out of the control room and into the neighboring locker room.

Siya opened a locker, then gestured at the stormsword on my belt. "Verona said to send you two into the maze without any weapons, since this is a test of your truebond connection and not your fighting skills. Instead of teaming up to battle an enemy like the House Battis Hammers, you and Vesper will be separated, and you'll be forced to communicate, find each other, and reach the center of the maze using only your bond."

My right hand dropped to the silver hilt of my stormsword, and my thumb stroked over a large sapphsidian jewel that was such a dark blue it almost looked black. The sapphsidian was shaped like an arrow, the sigil for House Caldaren, although

Vesper always claimed it looked more like a spade from an old-fashioned tarot or playing card. Other arrow sigils were also carved into the hilt, along with a few tiny stars, and there were several eyes that were a sign of my truebond with Vesper. Curls of silver stretched out in opposite directions to form the sword's crossguard, while still more curls of silver arced up to cup the base of the lunarium blade.

My fingers clenched around the hilt. The pale, opalescent lunarium glimmered with a dark blue light in a reflection of my psion power, and the entire sword vibrated slightly, like a cat purring against my palm, just waiting to be used.

"Come on, Kyrion," Siya said in a wheedling voice. "Nothing is going to happen to your precious sword."

I gave her a sour look, but I plucked the weapon off my belt and passed it over.

Siya slid the sword into the locker, then held her hand out to Vesper. "You too."

Vesper sighed, but she also plucked her stormsword off her belt and handed it to Siya. Vesper's weapon was a bit smaller than mine, and three sapphsidian jewels shaped like eyes adorned the silver hilt to indicate her seer power. Several arrows were also carved into the hilt in a reflection of our truebond, while the sword's pommel featured a sigil that could be interpreted as either *Z* for Zimmer or *N* for Nerezza, depending on which way you looked at it.

Asterin waggled her finger back and forth between Vesper and me. "Blasters and tablets too."

This time, Vesper and I both grumbled. She grabbed the blaster off her belt, while I fished mine out of the holster on my right thigh. We handed over our tablets, and I also removed the silver bandolier of supplies that was slung across my chest.

Siya stowed everything in the locker, then shut the door and placed her thumb on a scanner. A green light flashed, and the scanner beeped in confirmation.

"Just in case you get any ideas about trying to sneak a weapon into the maze, Arrow," Siya said, a chiding note creeping into her voice.

I clutched my chest in mock outrage just like Vesper had done earlier. "Would *I* do something like that?"

"Absolutely," Asterin and Siya replied in unison.

The two women froze and stared at each other. As children, they had been best friends until Asterin's father, Urston, was killed in a mining accident, along with Siya's uncle, Irzin. As a result, House Armas had been embroiled in wrongful-death lawsuits and gone bankrupt, so Verona, Asterin's mother, had started working for Siya's father, Aldrich, to help pay down her late husband's massive debts. Verona and Aldrich had eventually fallen in love, formed a truebond, and gotten married.

Asterin and Siya had been at odds ever since, and Vesper and I had only added to the stepsisters' conflict.

Two weeks ago, corporate mercenaries Esmina Reston and Pollux Lamont had attacked the Collier estate and kidnapped me to force Vesper to fix a design flaw in a powerful new hand cannon produced by the Techwave. Vesper had brought the weapon to Stardrop Falls, an abandoned mining museum with extensive caverns and an underground waterfall.

Vesper had willingly walked into the Serpens Corp mercenaries' trap, which had been orchestrated by Nerezza Blackwell. Eventually, Vesper and I had killed Esmina and Pollux, with Zane and Asterin's help. Nerezza had fled, of course, the way she always did when the fighting started and bodies started dropping.

Nerezza's spaceship had exploded shortly after takeoff, thanks to the bombs Esmina and Pollux had planted on board. No one had seen or heard from Nerezza since, but I was willing to bet the disgraced Regal lady was still alive and plotting against us once again.

Siya stared at Asterin a moment longer, then cleared her

throat. "I'm going to check with Jeffrey that the maze has been reset with the truebond training program."

Asterin frowned. "Didn't you already do that?"

Siya spun around on her heel and strode away like she hadn't heard the question.

Asterin watched her stepsister and former friend go with a neutral expression, although sharp needles of hurt wafted off her and stabbed my telempathy. I regretted causing more strife between Asterin and her family, but I would be dead if not for Vesper defying Lord Aldrich and all the other rogue actions she had taken to rescue me.

Vesper's soft sigh sounded in my mind. *Do you feel as bad as I do about this new rift between Asterin and Siya?*

Yes, but they'll figure it out. Just like we did with our true-bond.

Vesper gave me a warm smile, although it quickly melted away. She looked at Asterin, and the velvety ribbon of her in my mind hummed, as though she was trying to think of a way to fix our friends' relationship the same way she would repair a malfunctioning appliance in her research-and-development lab at Quill Corp.

I wished her luck, although I knew better than anyone else that some things just couldn't be fixed, especially all the harsh words and hard feelings that zipped back and forth between family members, damaging everyone in equal, brutal measure.

TWO

VESPER

Kyrion, Asterin, and I stayed in the locker room, waiting for Siya to return.

Kyrion raked a hand though his midnight-black hair, although the longish wavy locks fell right back into place. The overhead lights cast shadows on his pale skin and brought out his high cheekbones and sharp nose, along with the worried line that had taken up residence over his dark, ink-blue eyes.

Kyrion clasped his hands behind his back and started pacing, and the sticky cobweb of him in my mind bristled with nervous anticipation. Or maybe that was my own emotion sloshing around in my stomach. Sometimes it was hard to tell whether I was experiencing my own feelings, Kyrion's feelings, or a mixture of the two.

When Aldrich and Verona had first suggested we come to the training facility a few days ago, I had been excited for the challenge. But now that I had seen how massive the maze was . . . well, doubt had eclipsed my eagerness like a sun crossing in front of a moon.

Two weeks ago, when Kyrion and I defeated Esmina Reston and Pollux Lamont, we had finally stabilized and solidified our truebond. Eliminating the mercenaries had been a big relief, but the battle had also forced us to confront some of our deepest fears. I'd been worried I wasn't a skilled enough warrior to be bonded to Kyrion, while he'd been concerned he wasn't strong enough to protect me from our many enemies.

Kyrion and I were both still afraid of those things, but we could handle our fears much better than before. In a weird way, I was grateful to Esmina and Pollux for teaching us some important lessons about being equal partners and how Kyrion and I could rely on ourselves and our individual abilities, as well as each other and the truebond between us.

That mutual understanding and trust had sunk into our bond and made it even more powerful. Most of the time, I could use Kyrion's telekinesis and telepathy when and how I wanted, while he was learning to interpret my seer magic, which often appeared as silver flares of light around people or objects that were going to be useful or important in some future way. I still couldn't form a psionic blade, a weapon made of pure mental energy, on a regular basis like Kyrion, but I was getting better at summoning and wielding my seer magic, along with Kyrion's abilities. And we were both getting stronger, able to pull on more and more power without tiring ourselves or exhausting each other's abilities.

But the House Battis maze was quite literally the biggest challenge we had faced, and I was worried all the progress we'd made wasn't enough to help us navigate through the twists and turns, along with the obstacles hidden inside.

As a child, I always had to be *the best*—the best, most devoted student, who got the best and highest grades, who built the best and most elaborate projects for my science classes. I'd thought if only I was good, smart, and strong enough, I could eventually earn Nerezza's love. Of course, my duplicitous mother had no love to give, but I'd never been able to shake off that inner drive, dedication, and determination. Now I wanted—*needed*—to be the best warrior and truebonded partner possible for Kyrion's sake, so he wouldn't be either physically or psionically hurt by my actions.

Plus, I *hated* losing. I loved Kyrion with every atom of my being, but that didn't mean I wouldn't try my best to beat him in our friendly competition to see who could find the other and reach the center of the maze first.

My hand drifted down to the empty slot on my belt where my stormsword would normally be. Even though I had only been training with the weapon for a few months, it already felt like a part of me, and I missed its slight, comforting weight.

I studied the thumbprint scanner on the locker where Siya had stored our weapons. Quill Corp, my company, manufactured something similar, and my mind whirred, comparing those schematics to this device. It wouldn't be too hard to pry off the plastic cover, yank the wires free, and hot-wire the scanner to open the locker.

Asterin stepped in front of me, blocking my view of the scanner. She shook her right index finger back and forth. "Nuh-uh. None of that. No plotting how you can finesse the locker open and grab a weapon. That's an order from my mother."

I huffed out an annoyed breath. "*Fine.* Although if Verona wanted me to follow her orders, then she should have come with us and explained exactly how we're supposed to navigate the maze using just our truebond."

Asterin shrugged. "Verona and Aldrich had some business at another House. They'll meet us back at the estate later tonight. But they gave Siya and me strict instructions about your training, including not letting you and Kyrion take any weapons into the maze, especially not your stormswords."

"Why?" I asked.

"The lunarium blades could amplify your psionic abilities, instead of making you and Kyrion rely solely on your bond."

I grumbled, but Asterin gave me a serene smile that was an eerie match to the expression Lady Verona so often used to get her way.

Footsteps squeaked on the tile floor, and Siya stepped into view carrying two silver cuffs. "Here," she said, holding the cuffs out to Kyrion and me. "Put these on."

We did as she asked. The silver was surprisingly lightweight, and the cuff shrank a bit, automatically adjusting so that it fit snugly on my left wrist. A small holoscreen embedded in the metal flared to life, and a series of numbers appeared, showing my vital signs.

"What are these?" Kyrion asked in a suspicious voice.

"Holocuffs," Siya replied. "They are synced to the main panel in the control room and create holograms that Asterin and I can watch. The cuffs will also show us where you two are in the maze, what obstacles you encounter, and how much stress they put on your bodies."

I hummed in appreciation at the thought of analyzing all that data, but Kyrion glared at his cuff like he wanted to rip it off.

"What else will this device do?" he muttered. "Shock us if we don't reach the center of the maze quickly enough?"

Asterin frowned. "Of course not! Why would you even think that?"

"Holloway used such devices in the past," Kyrion replied in a stiff voice. "To *motivate* me during my Arrow training, especially when I was younger. There are always consequences for failure."

My heart squeezed. Kyrion was such a strong, accomplished warrior I sometimes forgot all the cruel, grueling things he had endured at Holloway's hands.

"No, the cuffs won't shock you," Siya replied. "But Lady Battis *will* charge House Collier for every single minute you go over the allotted time to reach the center of the maze."

Kyrion and I shared a wary look. Now there was even more pressure to complete the training as fast as possible.

More footsteps squeaked on the floor, and several people trooped into the locker room. They were a mix of men and women, all shapes and sizes, and ranging in age from early twenties to late sixties. All wore red House Battis uniforms stained with sweat and dirt and singed with minor blaster burns. One woman even had a couple of pink-star honeysuckle blossoms snagged in her long, tangled blond hair, making her look like a princess from some old fairy tale.

Every person was carrying at least one weapon. Mostly blasters and war hammers, along with a few hand cannons.

I studied the cannons, but they were an old, standard model by House Collier and not the new, much deadlier Techwave cannons that were based on my stolen design. I exhaled a quiet sigh of relief. Sooner or later, someone besides me was going to figure out how to fix the faulty Techwave cannons, but that was a worry for another day.

The men and women split off, going over to the other lockers or heading toward the shower stalls. None of them said a word, and they were all either limping, grimacing, or both.

More footsteps squeaked, and a tall man swaggered into view. His uniform was immaculate, and he was whistling instead of wincing. Ah, this must be the winning warrior.

The man was quite handsome, with longish wavy dark brown hair, dark brown eyes, and tan skin that practically glowed with health and vitality, as though he had just gone to a fancy spa. He looked to be in his late thirties, the same age as me, Kyrion, Asterin, and Siya. His body was all lean, hard muscle, and his high, sharp cheekbones, straight nose, and square jaw could have easily gotten him a modeling job on a fashion gossipcast.

Several daggers hung from his black leather belt, along with a blaster I recognized as a House Battis design. I sniffed.

A serviceable enough weapon, although it wasn't nearly as powerful and reliable as the new Quill Corp blaster I had been working on before Kyrion and I were forced to go on the run.

The man stopped and beamed at my friends. "Asterin! Siya!" he said in a deep baritone. "How wonderful to see you both again! It's been far too long."

Asterin stepped forward, smiling wide. "Hello, Roderick. It's good to see you too."

He returned Asterin's smile, then looked over at Siya. "Hello, Siya."

"Roderick," she replied in a cool voice, her face neutral.

Roderick's smile remained steady, although his eyes narrowed at the Erzton lady's less-than-warm welcome.

Asterin gestured at him. "This is Roderick Battis. He's the one who extended the invitation for your training and agreed to let us use the facility after hours." Next, she gestured at Kyrion and me. "This is Lord Kyrion Caldaren and Lady Vesper Quill from the Imperium."

"Of course," Roderick murmured. "I've seen them on the gossipcasts."

Kyrion's jaw clenched. As a Regal lord and the head of the Arrows, Kyrion had been a staple on the gossipcasts for years, but he had shot to a newfound level of notoriety thanks to our truebond.

Several weeks ago, Callus Holloway had tried to siphon off our truebond magic during a midnight ball at Crownpoint Palace. Kyrion and I had managed to create a storm of psionic lightning that had decimated the throne room, and then we had fought Imperium soldiers and Holloway's Bronze Hand guards before getting onto Kyrion's *Dream World* blitzer and flying away from the palace.

The Imperium gossipcasts had covered our escape with breathless glee, and in recent days, the Erzton gossipcasts had picked up the story, along with our battle against the Serpens

Corp mercenaries at the Stardrop Falls mining museum. By this point, everyone in the blasted galaxy probably knew exactly who Kyrion and I were.

As a lab rat, someone who had toiled away in the R&D departments of Regal corporations for years, I was used to being invisible. But going from lab rat to Regal lady to wanted fugitive over the last several months had exponentially raised my profile, and I was still struggling to deal with all the unwanted attention—and harsh judgment—that came along with being infamous.

Roderick bowed first to me, then to Kyrion. "It is a great pleasure to meet you both. I'm delighted Lady Verona accepted my offer to let the two of you use my facility. Of course, I saw you both a few weeks ago during the marriage mart at the House Collier antiques emporium, but I didn't get a chance to introduce myself."

The marriage mart was a revered Erzton tradition in which the resources of every noble lord and lady were put on display, from the smallest trust fund to the largest factory. Other Erzton lords and ladies then decided whom they wanted to court based on how beneficial—or not—those resources might be to their own Houses and families.

I'd been shocked and more than a little disgusted at how Erzton society reduced romantic relationships to business transactions, although Kyrion had said such things were also common in Imperium Regal society. I thought it would be terribly sad to be courted knowing people were more interested in my credits and resources than in my personality and skills.

Asterin's assets had been on display during the marriage mart, but no one had shown any interest in courting her, despite the many mineral rights she owned on various moons and planets. Apparently, suspicions and stigmas were still attached to Asterin, thanks to the supposed mining accident that had killed her father and bankrupted House Armas all those years ago.

Roderick smiled and glanced back and forth between Kyrion and me, clearly expecting us to continue the conversation. Neither of us said anything, and the lord's smile twisted into an annoyed scowl. Had Kyrion and I violated some Erzton social rule?

Roderick's gaze skated over me and landed firmly on Kyrion, and his scowl smoothed back out into a wide, happy smile, like he'd just met a beloved celebrity. He stared at Kyrion a moment longer, then looked at Asterin again. "I've been meaning to message you, Asterin. You simply *must* come on my next hunt. We're going to Frozon 15. Several packs of wolves and bears can be found on the moon, as well as some ice dragons and wyverns from the rumors I've heard. They should provide me with a decent challenge, for a change."

His dark brown eyes gleamed with excitement, and his thumb stroked over the hilt of a dagger on his belt.

Asterin's eyes lit up, and her face practically glowed with happiness. "That sounds wonderful!"

But just as quickly, her eyes dimmed, and a wistful look creased her features. "But I have so much work to do on my projects overseeing some new tourist attractions for the Regenwald Resort. Even if I could get away, I would probably just sit by the fire and drink Frozon hot chocolate instead of tromping around the snowy tundra."

Roderick's smile widened, and he leaned forward. "Oh, I'm sure I can convince you to come. You deserve a vacation, and I need someone to help me stay warm during the long, cold nights."

His voice dropped to a low, husky purr, and he winked at Asterin. A blush flared in her pale cheeks, and another wistful expression filled her face. Siya rolled her eyes, although neither Roderick nor Asterin noticed.

Roderick drew back and gestured at the House Battis Hammers who were opening their lockers and shrugging out of their dirty uniforms. "We're done for the evening. I have a few things to finish up in my office, but I'll leave Jeffrey behind to oversee the control room. But other than that, the four of you will have the facility to yourselves. Try not to go too crazy with your blasters, eh? We've already had to replace far too many flowers for my mother's liking this month."

Asterin laughed at his joke. Kyrion and I politely chuckled, but Siya remained silent. Roderick bowed to us all again, grinned at Asterin, and headed over to the other warriors.

"Come on," Siya muttered. "We only have the facility for two hours before they start charging us for extra time. Or have you forgotten that favors from House Battis always come with a hefty price tag?"

The warm glow snuffed out of Asterin's face. "How can I forget when you are constantly reminding me?"

Our two friends glared at each other, with Kyrion and me looking on in awkward silence.

Asterin glanced over at us. "In case it isn't already painfully obvious, Siya despises Roderick. She has ever since we were children."

Siya stiffened, her chin jutting up. "House Battis is a long-standing rival of House Collier. It is always wise to be wary of potential enemies."

Asterin crossed her arms over her chest. "Roderick is not the head of his House, and you're blaming him for things he doesn't have any control over."

"He has a lot more control than you think," Siya muttered. "He always has."

Asterin's face crinkled in confusion. She opened her mouth, but Siya sliced her hand through the air.

"Forget it," Siya muttered again. "It doesn't matter."

And you wouldn't believe me anyway. Siya's snide thought whispered through my mind.

I glanced at Asterin, but she glared at her stepsister like she hadn't heard Siya's inner musing. Asterin was a psion, just like

Siya and Kyrion, although I'd never been able to figure out exactly what abilities she had. Sometimes Asterin seemed like a strong psion, but other times she seemed to have no magic at all.

Asterin glared at Siya a moment longer, then jerked her head at Kyrion. "Come on, Kyrion. Let's get into position so that you and Vesper can enter the maze at the same time."

Kyrion's dark blue gaze locked with mine. "Meet you in the middle?"

"It's a date," I replied in a cheerful voice, echoing his earlier words.

A crooked grin curved the corner of Kyrion's mouth, and he and Asterin left the locker room.

Siya glanced over her shoulder at Roderick, who was smiling, laughing, and joking with his friends. Siya's nostrils flared with disgust, and she stomped toward the exit.

I followed her, growing more and more curious about the history between the Erzton nobles. Being wary of someone from a rival House was one thing, but Siya clearly had a deep, personal dislike of Roderick. Why? What had he done to her?

As we rounded a row of lockers, I looked back over my shoulder. Roderick snapped his fingers at the Hammers in a sharp, impatient rhythm. The other warriors quickly gathered around, and the Erzton lord started speaking in a low, hushed voice. Roderick had been nothing but polite, but something about his sudden furtiveness made me uneasy.

"Let's go, Vesper," Siya muttered, quickening her pace. "The sooner you and Kyrion get through the maze, the sooner we can leave."

I followed her out of the locker room, but my unease trailed along behind me like a shadow I couldn't escape.

Siya marched through the corridors in silence, her shoulders squared, her spine ramrod straight. Even without Kyrion's telempathy, I still would have been able to sense exactly how annoyed, tense, and frustrated she was.

"What's the real reason you dislike Roderick Battis?" I asked. "It's obviously a lot more serious than just him belonging to a rival House."

Siya's face tightened with anger. "You're assuming there is only one reason."

"Then tell me all the reasons."

Siya stopped, spun toward me, and slapped her hands on her hips. "You want to know about Roderick? Well, for starters, he was the first boy Asterin ever had a crush on when we were teenagers, so she's always had a blind spot where he is concerned."

"What kind of blind spot?"

Siya laughed, but it was a bitter sound. "Asterin invited Roderick to a society ball, and she was so excited when he said yes. Then the mining accident happened, and Asterin's father and my uncle were killed. A few days later, right after the funerals, Roderick told Asterin that he couldn't go to the ball with her."

I grimaced. "That's harsh."

Siya nodded. "He blamed his parents, said they made him back out because they didn't want House Battis to get dragged into the lawsuits between House Armas and the other Houses. But I knew the *truth*."

"Which was?"

"Asterin didn't have the money, power, and support of a major House anymore. That's the *real* reason Roderick dropped her. But Asterin forgave him for that, just like she always forgives him for anything and everything and explains away all his actions, no matter how rude and thoughtless they are."

Siya finally ran out of clipped, angry words. Her hands slipped off her hips, and she shook her head, more disgust crinkling her face. "And that's not even the worst thing Roderick has done."

"What is the worst thing?"

Siya shifted on her feet, torn between telling or keeping the secret. She stilled and let out a tense breath. "Asterin and Roderick started dating a few months before Asterin went to a university on a Temperate planet to study mining. She asked Roderick to go with her, but he was already enrolled at a university here on Sygnustern, so they agreed to a long-distance relationship."

"Let me guess. Roderick cheated on Asterin."

Siya nodded. "Multiple times."

My heart ached for my friend—and for myself.

Once upon a time, I had dated a man named Conrad Fawley, who had cheated on me with Sabine Kent, a Regal lady. Conrad had tossed me aside like a piece of trash to climb the Regal ladder, and he'd also stolen my weapons, spaceships, and other designs and given them to Rowena Kent, Sabine's mother and the head of Kent Corp. Conrad had also gone along with Rowena's scheme to kill me and crash Imperium ships on command for the Techwave. Eventually, Conrad's crimes had caught up to him, and he'd died in Imperium custody, along with the Kents.

Conrad might have fallen victim to karma, fate, destiny, or whatever force balanced the galactic scales of justice, but he'd still left a deep, jagged scar on my heart. I would never forget his casual cruelty, but the painful experience had made me even more grateful that I'd found Kyrion, someone I could always fully, completely trust, truebond or not.

"Did Asterin ever find out about Roderick's cheating?" I asked.

"No," Siya replied in a sharp voice. "Things were already strained between us, and I didn't want to push her away completely, so I kept quiet. A few months later, Roderick was sent to manage House Battis assets on another planet, and their relationship finally fizzled out."

She chewed on her lower lip, and a wave of guilt surged off her, strong enough to make my own stomach churn.

"But cheating still isn't the worst thing Roderick did," I guessed.

Siya blinked in surprise. "No. While Asterin was away, I saw Roderick at a party, and he started flirting with me. Said he'd always liked me ever since we were kids, and we could do great things for our Houses together now that we were older."

My eyebrows shot up. I hadn't known Siya Collier for long, but one of the things I most admired was her fierce loyalty to her House, family, and friends. She would *never* betray Asterin like that, something Roderick should have known.

Siya's lips curled back into a derisive sneer. "As if I couldn't see right through that pompous fool. Roderick Battis only cares about his own House and ambitions. And don't even get me started on those ridiculous trips he goes on every few months."

I thought of his earlier words. "Roderick goes to Frozon moons and other planets and hunts creatures?"

Such excursions were common in the Imperium, and I'd seen more than one gossipcast reporter follow a Regal lord or lady through a Tropics rain forest in search of tigers, dragons, and other large, dangerous predators. I suppose when you had more credits than you could ever spend, you needed some sort of challenge—even if it came with an alarming number of razor-sharp teeth and claws.

Siya nodded. "The more exotic and dangerous the creature, the better. He even has their heads stuffed and mounted. There's an entire hall in Castle Battis devoted to Roderick's *trophies*." Her lips curled back with even more disgust. "Roderick's hunts are cruel and barbaric, just like he is, but Asterin only sees what she wants to see."

"Why?"

Siya sighed. "I think Roderick reminds Asterin of a time when she was extremely happy."

"Before her father died."

Siya nodded. "Asterin adored her father, which is why she's still convinced Urston isn't to blame for the mining accident." She shook her head and let out a tense breath. "But Asterin won't listen about her father or Roderick. She *never* listens to me about anything important."

"I'm sorry your relationship is so strained."

Anger flared in Siya's hazel eyes, making them shimmer brightly. "You should be sorry, Vesper. Things were finally getting better between Asterin and me, but then you and Zane Zimmer dragged her into your scheme to rescue Kyrion from the Serpens Corp mercenaries. You went against my father's orders, and your rogue actions almost got Asterin killed, along with the rest of you."

After we'd rescued Kyrion from Stardrop Falls, Siya and Asterin had gotten into a heated argument in a garden at the Collier estate. I hadn't heard everything they'd said, but the two women had barely spoken to each other over the last several days.

"Asterin decided to help Zane and me of her own free will," I replied. "Just like she helped Kyrion and me battle the Techwave at the Regenwald Resort and then escape from Crownpoint Palace. If you think anyone can drag Asterin Armas into anything she doesn't want to do, then you don't know her as well as you think."

Siya's right hand clenched around the war hammer on her belt, and green magic sparked, crackled, and hissed around the lunarium weapon, mirroring her anger.

My seer magic whispered a warning, but I gave Siya a cool look. Over the past few months, I had faced down one vicious enemy after another, and I wasn't about to let the Hammer intimidate me. Especially since I would have gone rogue and done the exact same things again right now if Kyrion was in danger.

Siya removed her hand from the hammer. Her green magic vanished, although she kept glaring at me. "Let's get this over with. The sooner you and Kyrion learn to fully control your truebond, the sooner the two of you can leave Sygnustern and take your problems back to the Imperium."

She brushed past me and strode down the corridor. I blew out a tense breath and followed the warrior, but the harsh, uncomfortable truth of her words pounded through my body with every step.

Siya was right. My rogue actions had already caused a multitude of problems for her and Asterin. But the most worrisome thing was my seer magic, which kept whispering that only more troubles were on the way for us all.

THREE

VESPER

Siya shoved through a door and stomped down a set of spiral stairs. The sharp, twisting curve reminded me of going down similar stairs into my mindscape, the place deep inside my mind, body, and heart where my seer magic resided.

Siya stopped at the bottom of the stairs and entered a code into a keypad. A light turned green, and she yanked the door open.

We stepped out onto the ground floor. From the upper level, the maze had looked relatively simple. But down here, the metal walls jutted up like a ring of silver teeth covered with the thick green film of the honeysuckle vines. The light was dim and murky, and the only sound was the faint hum of the facility's ventilation system. A finger of unease slid down my spine, then plummeted into the sloshing sea of nervous energy that had flooded my stomach.

Siya walked over to a long metal panel bristling with lights, buttons, and levers just like the one Jeffrey had been operating in the control room. She bent down and started typing on a holoscreen. The lights hanging over the maze flashed in response, accepting her commands.

"You'll enter the maze here, while Kyrion will enter from the opposite side. Then you'll both be sealed inside," Siya explained. "The goal is to use your truebond to communicate with Kyrion and find him in the center, no matter what physical obstacles get in your way. Verona suggested picturing the training exercise like you and Kyrion are two magnets that are slowly being drawn together. The closer you get, the stronger your connection should be until ... *smack!*" She clapped her hands together, and I jumped at the sharp sound. "The two of you meet in the middle."

I nodded. "Magnets. Got it. What sort of obstacles are in the maze?"

"That's for you and Kyrion to discover. But the obstacles are designed to test your truebond and see how easily you and Kyrion can use both your own and each other's psionic abilities." Siya tilted her head toward the maze. "Although I will warn you that the maze is equipped with psionic dampeners and sensory-deprivation tools that deliberately make it difficult for bonded couples to tap into their connection."

This would be a true test of how much progress Kyrion and I had made over the past two weeks. When the Serpens Corp mercenaries captured Kyrion, I hadn't been able to sense his thoughts and feelings through our bond, and that aching emptiness had been one of the most hopeless, sickening things I'd ever experienced. Plus, it was just a matter of time before Callus Holloway, Nerezza, or the Techwave targeted us again. If the worst happened, and Kyrion and I were separated, this training might help me find him, or vice versa.

Kyrion had been right in the locker room. There were always consequences for failure, and ours could be imprisonment—or worse. The sloshing sea in my stomach rocked a little more violently.

"And if we can't communicate and find each other using our bond? Or reach the center of the maze?"

Siya shrugged. "Asterin and I will be watching from the control room, along with Jeffrey, but you aren't fighting other warriors, so you won't get mock-killed, disqualified, and have to leave the maze like the House Battis Hammers we watched earlier. Instead, you and Kyrion will stay in the maze until you either find each other or admit defeat. Either way, Asterin and I won't open the exits and pull you out unless absolutely necessary."

I blinked in surprise. "Is it ever necessary to pull people out?"

"Training accidents happen from time to time, especially when alpha Hammers and other hotshot warriors think they are stronger and more powerful than they actually are." Siya arched a chiding eyebrow. "So don't do anything too stupid and reckless, okay, Vesper?"

I winced. *Stupid* and *reckless* could have been my middle names, given all the near-death experiences Kyrion and I had had over the past several months.

Siya must have sensed my worry with her telempathy because she snorted. "It's a training facility, Vesper. You might get a few bumps and bruises or fall and twist your ankle, but you're not going to *die*. All the blasters and other weapons are set to stun. Of course, something could always malfunction, but at the worst, you might get a few mild burns or a bit of frostbite from the harsher biodome environments."

I gave her a triumphant smile. "Aha! So there *are* blasters hidden in the maze."

Siya scowled. "You're not as clever as you think for figuring that out."

"And your lips aren't as tightly sealed as *you* think," I crowed back.

She rolled her eyes. "Just do us all a favor and try to get through the maze as quickly as possible."

"So the time element is important too." My mind churned. "I'm guessing the faster we get through the maze, the higher we score. And if we reach the center more quickly than the other bonded couples, that will mean our bond is the strongest of all the ones that have been measured. Right?"

"Something like that," Siya replied, still being deliberately vague. "But I'd also like to be home before midnight and not give Roderick Battis any more credits than absolutely necessary."

I opened my mouth to snipe back, but Siya stabbed a finger at me.

"Most important of all, do *not* embarrass House Collier. We already have enough problems without you and Kyrion toppling the walls, destroying the biodomes, or doing something else foolish and costly to piss off House Battis."

I snapped up my hand in a mock salute. "Yes, ma'am!"

Siya huffed and fiddled with the controls again. More lights flashed on the panel and over the maze itself. A faint hiss also sounded, although I couldn't tell what it was or where it was coming from.

Siya hit a final button, and several green lights lit up in a row on the panel. The soft, steady *squeak-squeak-squeak* of wheels sounded, and a metal wall skated back on a track, revealing the closest maze entrance, which was about the size of a wide door.

There was nothing overtly sinister about the opening, but another finger of unease slid down my spine. "This place gives me the creeps."

"It's supposed to give you the creeps," Siya replied. "That's what we're paying for."

Kyrion and I had been awarded a sizeable, long-standing bounty for taking down Esmina Reston and Pollux Lamont, so we had offered to foot the bill for the training, but Aldrich and Verona had declined. House Collier already had a deal in place with House Battis, so the Colliers had added our session to their tab. The Colliers' generosity was another reason I was determined to conquer the maze. I didn't want Aldrich and Verona to have spent their money for nothing.

The holoscreen embedded in the control panel let out a loud beep, and Siya checked the message. "Jeffrey says that Asterin and Kyrion are in position and ready to begin." She made a shooing gesture with her hand. "Enter the maze, and I'll close the door behind you."

I stared at the opening again. For once, my seer magic was quiet, and no telltale silver flares of light appeared to hint at possible danger, but I still felt like something was wrong.

Over the last several months, I'd learned to trust my instincts, since they were right more often than not. I opened my mouth to call off the training, but after a few seconds, I mashed my lips shut. Lord Aldrich and Lady Verona had gone to a lot of trouble—and forked over a lot of credits—to arrange this opportunity, and I didn't want to disappoint them. I also didn't want Roderick to charge the Colliers extra if Kyrion and I didn't finish the maze in the allotted time.

And the petty, selfish part of me also wanted to prove Siya wrong, since she clearly thought Kyrion and I wouldn't be able to master the maze. But most important of all, I wanted to prove to Kyrion and myself that our bond was growing stronger and that we could do anything together.

"See you soon," I said.

Siya lifted her hand to her forehead and mimicked my mocking salute. Then she made another little shooing motion, like I was a dog she was nudging into a kennel.

I turned away from her, strode over to the maze, and stopped at the entrance. Pink-star honeysuckle vines clung to the tall metal walls on either side of a gray stone path. Once again, I didn't see anything sinister, but those cold fingers of unease kept tickling my spine.

"Anytime, Vesper," Siya drawled.

I swallowed the knot of nerves in my throat and moved forward.

As soon as I stepped into the maze, a sharp, tingling sensation swept over my skin, like I had just walked through an energy shield. I stopped. The intense tingling faded away, although my skin kept prickling, as though I was about to give myself a violent static shock. A dull noise also sounded, like water roaring in my ears. The psionic dampeners and sensory-deprivation devices must have activated when I entered the maze.

I looked over my shoulder through the opening. Siya gave me a thumbs-up, then hit a button on the control panel. Another series of *squeak-squeak-squeaks* rang out, and the metal wall slid back into place, locking me inside the maze.

FOUR

KYRION

Asterin didn't say anything as she led me through several corridors, but anger and tension radiated off her like heat from a Tropics sun.

I considered asking Asterin if she wanted to talk about her latest argument with Siya, but I decided against it. I knew better than anyone that talking simply wouldn't—*couldn't*—fix some things, especially when it came to messy, complicated familial relationships. All my talking had never roused my father out of his grief after my mother died or convinced Chauncey just how much I needed him. I didn't know what, if any, comfort I could offer Asterin now, especially since Vesper's and my arrival had created even more problems between my friend and her stepsister.

Asterin marched down some steps, then punched in a code on a keypad. The door buzzed open, and the two of us stepped through to the other side. In front of us, the maze loomed up and out like a mushroom cloud about to swallow everything in its vicinity. Admiration pulsed through me, along with more than a little wariness.

I let out a low whistle. "It is truly impressive."

Asterin's shoulders relaxed back and down, and some of her anger and tension drained away. "Roderick and his family never do anything halfway or on the cheap. It took them years to design and build the maze, but now it's the largest, most sophisticated and comprehensive training facility on Sygnustern."

Pride rippled through her voice, and I thought of how her face had softened whenever she looked at Roderick. The two of them had obviously been involved, although I wasn't going to pry into their relationship, especially since Roderick seemed to be another point of contention between Asterin and Siya.

Asterin moved over to a control panel positioned in front of one of the maze entrances.

I trailed along behind her. "Have you ever trained here?"

Asterin nodded and started hitting buttons on the panel. "Several times. All members of House Collier are required to go through basic combat training when they turn eighteen, along with refresher courses every two years. That includes everyone from the chefs at the Collier estate, to the account managers in the mineral exchanges in the city, to the heavy-equipment operators in the shipping yard. Folks who join House Collier later in life are also required to complete the training. And of course, Siya and the other House Collier Hammers and guards come here every other month to plan and prepare for various doomsday scenarios."

"Like an army of mercenaries invading the Collier estate?" I asked in a sardonic tone.

Asterin blanched at the reminder of the recent attack by Esmina Reston, Pollux Lamont, and their Serpens Corp mercenaries. "Exactly like that."

Asterin turned her attention back to the control panel and yanked on a few levers. The sharp, wrenching motions matched the churning of guilt in my gut. Esmina and Pollux had a long-standing feud with Aldrich and Verona Collier and a burning desire to destroy their House, but Vesper and me staying at the Collier estate had played a large part in the mercenaries deciding to attack, and several people had been killed as a result. Vesper and I had been searching for a safe haven, but we had ended up with blood on our hands. I just wondered how much more innocent blood would be spilled before we killed our enemies—or they killed us.

I sighed and scrubbed a hand through my hair. Asterin glanced over at me, as though she could feel my guilt. Perhaps she could with whatever psion powers she had.

"Where will you and Siya be while Vesper and I are in the maze?"

Asterin jerked her thumb over her shoulder. "Upstairs in the control room with Jeffrey. All three of us will monitor your progress, along with your vital signs."

I poked my right index finger into the silver holocuff on my left wrist, jiggling the embedded holoscreen. My heart rate was climbing in proportion to my growing annoyance. I despised personal monitoring devices even more than I did cameras.

"After he finishes his work, Roderick will probably join us in the control room," Asterin continued. "Roderick says that studying other warriors, especially folks like you and Vesper who have never experienced the maze before, gives him and the technicians ideas for new and more challenging obstacles and environments."

Her voice practically hummed as she sang Roderick's praises, and her eyes sparkled with warmth. Asterin noticed my curious stare, and a blush stained her pale cheeks. "Roderick is an old friend."

I arched an eyebrow. "*Old friend?* Is that what you call it in the Erzton?"

Her blush burned a little brighter and hotter. "Roderick and I have . . . dated a few times over the years. In many ways, he was my first love."

Asterin's gaze grew distant, and her lips curved into a fond, dreamy smile. Suddenly, a silver light flared, and a second version of Asterin appeared, hovering in the air like a hologram. This second Asterin was only a teenager, and she was wearing a long frilly dress and twirling back and forth, like she was practicing a dance in front of a mirror.

I blinked. The second, teenage Asterin vanished, and it took me a moment to focus on the real woman in front of me. Vesper's seer power flared up when I least expected, and I was still getting used to the odd visions it showed me from time to time.

Asterin's gaze sharpened, and the dreamy smile plummeted from her lips. "But Siya has never liked Roderick, not even when we were children. She claims Roderick only cares about himself." Asterin shook her head. "Siya just doesn't understand that Roderick has certain duties as the heir of House Battis and that those duties sometimes conflict with what's best for House Collier."

Two weeks ago, during the marriage mart, Siya had told me how proud she was to serve House Collier—and how much always putting her House and people first weighed on her. Siya knew *exactly* how demanding being an heir was, but I held my tongue. Vesper and I had already caused enough tension between our friends without my jabbing my thumb into the sore spot Roderick Battis represented between Asterin and Siya.

A holoscreen embedded in the panel beeped, drawing Asterin's attention. "Jeffrey says Siya and Vesper are in position on the opposite side of the maze."

As if in response to her words, the metal wall blocking the maze entrance rolled back. Through the opening, a gray stone path led straight ahead like an arrow pointing toward unknown dangers. My gut churned again, this time with a mixture of jangling anticipation and nauseating dread.

When Lady Verona had first suggested the training exercise a few days ago, I'd been eager to prove how much progress

Vesper and I had made, not just in using our bond and respective psion powers but in trusting ourselves and each other and especially in dealing with our fears. But standing in front of the maze hammered home just what a massive challenge this truly was.

Cold, familiar doubt flooded my chest, making my inner monster whimper, but I clenched my jaw and ignored the noise. Conquering the maze was a necessary step, not just for training but to prove to Vesper and myself that we could handle all the dangerous enemies circling around us like sharks trailing the scent of blood in a Tropics ocean.

"Obstacles are hidden along the paths and in the biodomes, many of which have extreme climates that are dangerous in and of themselves," Asterin said. "The maze also features psionic dampeners and other equipment that will make it difficult for you and Vesper to use your telepathy to talk to each other."

"I would expect nothing less," I murmured.

Asterin waved a hand at the maze. "Everything in there is designed to draw your focus, use up your energy—physical, mental, and psionic—and disrupt your bond, just like a real-world enemy would do everything possible to keep you and Vesper apart. How fast it takes the two of you to find each other will indicate how quickly you can identify and solve problems, both as individuals and as a couple."

I looked at the towering walls. "And I'm guessing that Vesper and I using our psionic abilities along the way should also help us understand how much psion power we can pull from each other without completely draining each other's energy and abilities."

Vesper and I had already been testing those limits, but so far, our collective well of power was much deeper than I had ever imagined it could be.

"Yes," Asterin replied. "The training should give us a baseline of how strong your bond is compared to other bonded couples who have also been through the maze."

"Sounds like it will be a real challenge," I drawled, "in every sense of the word."

Asterin nodded. "That's the idea. Good luck, Kyrion."

"Thank you." I nodded back at her, then squared my shoulders, strode forward, and stepped into the maze.

The instant my boots touched the gray stone path, electricity crashed over my body like a tidal wave. I jerked to a halt. The uncomfortable sensation crackled across my skin for several seconds before dying down to an annoying hum. Psionic dampeners always made me feel like mosquitoes were whining in my ears.

More doubt flooded my chest, but I swatted it aside. The purpose of training was to hone your abilities and push your mind, body, and psionic powers to their utmost limits. Our enemies wouldn't show us any mercy, and Vesper and I had to be at our best and ready to protect ourselves, especially against Callus Holloway.

We needed a fresh challenge to keep us on our toes, and I was determined to overcome every obstacle in the maze, just as I had vowed in the cold depths of my heart to do whatever was necessary to protect Vesper—no matter what it cost me.

I glanced back over my shoulder and waved at Asterin. She returned the gesture, then hit another button on the panel. The metal wall rolled forward, blocking the exit and sealing me inside the maze.

FIVE

VESPER

I walked along the path, studying the dark gray flagstones underfoot, the dense honeysuckle vines covering the metal walls, and the domed ceiling high above. I couldn't be certain, given the distance, but it looked like it was snowing even more heavily than before outside. A strange, uncomfortable weight dropped over me, as though I could feel the cold, wet press of the snow despite the thick solar panels. I shivered and moved on.

The entry path shot straight into the maze, and I walked about a hundred feet before it branched off in three directions. Each path looked the same, and I didn't spot any obvious traps. Two paths curved in opposite directions, but I needed to find Kyrion in the center, so I took the path that led straight ahead.

Despite my desire to find Kyrion as quickly as possible and score well on the time element, I moved slowly, stopping every few feet to look and listen and examine everything through the lens of my seer magic. Nothing moved or stirred, and even the pink-star honeysuckle blossoms were frozen in place on their green vines.

The deeper I went into the maze, the more I noticed a soft, steady hiss that was just a little bit louder than the scraping of my boots on the flagstones. I stopped, wondering if I had tripped a hidden trap, but everything was the same as before. Flagstones underfoot, vines and walls on either side of the path, snow covering the domed ceiling high above.

I kept glancing around, and a tiny wink of silver caught my eye. Off to the left, a metal nozzle jutted out of the wall, almost completely hidden by the vines. The hissing grew louder, and white clouds spewed out of the nozzle.

I tensed, wondering if the clouds contained knockout gas or another hazard, but condensation quickly beaded on the honeysuckle blossoms, ran down the pink petals, and dripped onto the path. I exhaled. It was just water.

The nozzle spewed out more vapor clouds, which quickly drifted out and down and settled along the path. Within seconds, the area in front of me was cloaked with dense white fog, making it hard to see what lay ahead. The dampness added a sharp chill to the air, and I shivered, despite my tempered-silk clothes.

I lifted my hand and reached for Kyrion's telekinesis to sweep the fog aside, but to my surprise, I couldn't grasp his power.

Ever since I had rescued Kyrion from the Serpens Corp mercenaries, I had been able to use his abilities much more easily than before, although I still wasn't nearly as precise, skilled, and powerful as he was. But here in the maze, Kyrion seemed far, far away, like he was on a different planet. His telekinesis was shrouded in the same fog that was covering everything in a white mist, and I couldn't quite find it through the cool haze. I felt like I was trapped in a dim, distant dream and struggling to wake up and find my way back to him.

I'd experienced this same sort of odd, muffled disconnect

when Esmina Reston had injected Kyrion with chemicals that had disrupted our truebond when she kidnapped him from the Collier estate. Unease simmered in my stomach at the eerie similarity.

Instead of reaching blindly for Kyrion's telekinesis through the mental fog, I focused on the bond itself. The sticky little cobweb that was Kyrion's presence in my mind, body, and heart was anchored firmly in place, and the threads were bristling with tension. I was still connected to Kyrion, and our bond was as strong and solid as ever, no matter what tricks the white fog and psionic dampeners were playing on my senses.

Above my head, a soft whir sounded, and a black camera dropped down, swiveled around, and focused on me.

I looked directly into the lens. "You're going to have to do better than a little fog."

The red lights on the front remained bright and steady, staring at me like judgmental eyes. I snapped up my hand in a mock salute and walked on.

I eased along the path, once again looking and listening. If I were Jeffrey, the maze technician, I would use the fog to hide another, more challenging obstacle, since I couldn't avoid a trap I couldn't see.

But where would I place such a trap? The vine-covered walls on either side of the path were too obvious and still fairly easy to see, even with the fog. I doubted the camera tracking my movements would detach itself from the ceiling and crash down on my head, so that left only one option: the ground.

I dropped my gaze to the flagstones, and an almost imperceptible shimmer of motion caught my eye a few feet ahead. I stopped, crouched down, and took a better look. Tiny droplets of water had beaded up and were slowly dripping from a thin filament strung at ankle height across the flagstones.

A trip wire. Clever. I wouldn't have noticed it at all if not for the water condensation.

I stood up, moved forward, and stepped over the trip wire. I gingerly put my feet down on the other side, then waited. If I were Jeffrey, I would have rigged this area too, and I half expected the flagstone to depress under my boots.

A second passed. Then three . . . five . . . ten . . .

Nothing happened, and my breath escaped in a relieved rush. Apparently, Jeffrey wasn't as clever, devious, and diabolical as I was. Despite my nerves, disappointment flickered through me. I might hate losing, but it was no fun winning when things were this easy. I wanted the satisfaction of conquering a true challenge, of being, well, *the best*.

I moved forward. Up ahead, a couple of flagstones were cracked, like something large and heavy had slammed into them. Strange. I skirted around the broken chunks of stone, and my elbow brushed up against the honeysuckle vines on the right side of the path.

Click.

Something activated inside the greenery. I stopped and glanced around, wondering what trap I had just tripped.

Up ahead, a figure appeared on the path, heading in this direction. I squinted through the dense clouds of fog, trying to make out who it was.

Kyrion? I called out telepathically.

No answer. The figure came closer, but instead of morphing into a recognizable person, it grew darker, as though it was congealing into a solid shadow. Oversize green eyes snapped open, casting out shockingly bright glows. The eyes loomed closer, and the surrounding white fog took on the same eerie green tinge.

A wide, strong body made of black polyplastic armor appeared and combined with the glowing eyes to give the figure a disjointed, insectoid shape. But this was no imaginary monster on a horror serial—it was a Black Scarab, one of the Techwave's deadly automated troops.

My eyes widened, and my breath caught in my throat. I stood there, frozen in place, but then my mind kicked back into gear, and determination burned through my shock. I reached for the stormsword on my belt . . . but my hand only sliced through empty air. Drat. I'd forgotten that Siya had confiscated our weapons.

My gaze dropped to the ground, and I crouched down and snatched up a fist-size chunk from one of the broken flagstones. I stood up and cocked my arm back. The stone wasn't much of a weapon, and it wouldn't even scratch the automated troop's armor, but it was all I had to defend myself. Any second, the Scarab was going to spot me through the fog and sprint in this direction, its heavy feet clanking with every step . . .

Wait. Black Scarabs weren't exactly quiet, given their tall, hulking frames. Why wasn't I *already* hearing its clanking footsteps? Suspicion filled me.

The Scarab kept coming, heading down the center of the path. At this point, the machine was so close its eyes encased me in their eerie green glow, but instead of running away, I held my position off to the side of the path. My fingers clenched even tighter around the broken stone, and I held my arm up and ready, just in case my suspicion was wrong.

The Scarab came closer still, and my gaze locked on the buglike facets in its eyes, which glittered like neon emeralds. I held my position and braced myself to fight . . .

The Black Scarab walked right past me. It took a few more silent steps, and then its form dissolved into nothingness as it crossed the trip wire on the path behind me.

I stood there, my arm still cocked back and the chunk of stone still clenched in my fingers. A second passed. Then three . . . five . . . ten . . .

Nothing happened. My hand plummeted to my side, and a low, shaky laugh escaped from my lips. The Black Scarab was just a hologram, just an illusion.

I laughed again. I'd been wrong before. Jeffrey *was* just as clever, devious, and diabolical as I was. He'd activated the Black Scarab hologram to make me panic, whirl around, and run straight into the trip wire I'd already spotted and avoided, thus triggering the accompanying trap after all.

I glanced up at the camera hovering overhead and gave it a respectful nod. "Well played."

The red lights glowed steadily, but the camera lens opened and closed, almost as if Jeffrey was acknowledging my compliment from his perch in the control room.

I wiped the clammy sweat off my forehead, then studied the path up ahead. No more Black Scarab holograms appeared, although even more fog cloaked the area than before, intensifying the damp chill in the air.

I started to drop the stone, but then I thought better of it. I might be trapped in the maze without any weapons, but that didn't mean I couldn't create my *own* weapons, just like when I rigged different blasters together to make one much more powerful device. A fist-size rock wasn't all that powerful, but it was better than nothing.

I slid the broken stone into my pocket and headed even deeper into the maze.

SIX

VESPER

A minute later, the last of the fog wisped away, and I came to another junction where the path split off in three directions. Once again, all the paths looked the same, so I closed my eyes and reached for the sticky cobweb of Kyrion in my mind.

He hadn't whispered any telepathic thoughts to me, and he didn't seem to have heard me call out earlier, but his presence was still firmly anchored in my mind. Instead of trying to use his telepathy, I focused on Kyrion himself, on his strength and vitality. My feet moved of their own accord, and I turned toward that warmth like a blue-moon peony turning its face toward the sun.

I opened my eyes. The right path lay in front of me, so I took it.

Overhead, the camera moved along with me, while the holocuff on my left wrist continued to show my heart rate and other vital signs. Slow and steady, just like my progress through the maze.

I explored one path after another, trying to move closer to Kyrion. I didn't spot or trigger any more trip wires or holograms, although a couple of times, I had to backtrack from dead ends.

After a few more twists and turns, the path opened into a large circular biodome that resembled a Tropics rain forest. Rows of verdant green palm trees embedded in real dirt soared up into the air, along with smaller hibiscus trees and shrubs sporting bright magenta-, violet-, and daffodil-colored blossoms. Long black, green, and gray vines swooped from one tree to another, while small black lizards with colorful orange stripes lounged on several large rocks. Even a few frogs croaked somewhere deep in the shrubbery. An energy shield shimmered above, creating a clear bubble over the entire biodome.

I moved back and forth across the threshold. On the path side, the air was dry and chilly, but in the biodome, it was as humid and warm as a real Tropics rain forest. My admiration for Jeffrey and the other technicians rose several notches. Even with solar panels, it would still take an immense amount of energy—and a staggering number of credits—to climate-control the many biodomes in the maze. Asterin had been right about House Battis having money to burn.

The centerpiece of the biodome was an enormous bronze cauldron shaped like a hibiscus blossom. The metal petals stretched out more than six feet, while gas-powered flames in the base of the cauldron danced high into the air.

I squinted at the flames, wondering if they were a hologram, but heat blasted off the cauldron and warmed my cheeks, and curls of smoke wafted through the air and stung my eyes. Definitely *not* a hologram. The lit cauldron had to be an obstacle, just like the fog disguising the trip wire earlier.

The main path through the biodome split off into two walkways that circled around the cauldron. Foot-high statues shaped like black lizards were nestled in beds of pale orange pebbles along both walkways, and I had to do a double take to make sure the lizards were statues and not real creatures like the smaller ones still lounging on the rocks.

Instead of moving deeper into the biodome, I crouched down and scooped up a couple of pebbles. Then I stood up and tossed one of the orange stones onto the path that wound around the right side of the cauldron.

The pebble skittered across a few of the flagstones before rolling to a stop. I held my breath, but nothing happened. Hmm. Maybe I was wrong about the cauldron being a trap.

I tossed another pebble onto the path that wound around the left side of the cauldron. The pebble skipped along, then spun to a stop on a flagstone. A few orange sparks spewed up into the air, like the pebble had crossed through an energy shield. I frowned. Why would there be a shield that low to the ground—

WHOOSH!

A large jet of fire shot out from a nozzle tucked between two bronze petals in the base of the cauldron. Even though I had been expecting something to happen, I still yelped and jerked back in surprise.

The fire zipped directly across the path and slammed into the hibiscus trees and shrubs on the far side. The flames exploded out and up, cracking the branches and incinerating a wide swath of the bright blossoms. In an instant, singed petals drifted through the air like neon pink, purple, and yellow snowflakes.

My eyes widened in shock, and my heart leaped up into my throat. The flowers' sweet scent took on a charred aroma, and I had to swallow a sneeze.

First the hologram Scarab, now the booby-trapped path. The obstacles were far more lifelike—and dangerous—than Asterin and Siya had suggested. The jet of fire wouldn't have killed me, but I still would have been seriously injured—too injured to continue any further.

Ominous butterflies fluttered in my stomach, matching the cascade of charred petals. Did Siya and the other House Collier

Hammers use such hazardous obstacles when they trained? Or was this part of the special truebond program Aldrich and Verona had set up for Kyrion and me? But how would dousing me with flames help me learn more about or strengthen my connection to Kyrion?

I glanced up. Maybe it was a quirk of my seer magic, but instead of a silent, neutral observer, the overhead camera now seemed like a sinister, sentient robot patiently waiting to see what I would do next.

Asterin had said that Jeffrey was responsible for the obstacles, which meant the technician had deliberately made that jet of fire hot, wide, and powerful enough to burn and incapacitate me. Was Jeffrey trying to force me to quit? Was that part of his job? Either way, the fire was a vivid, painful example of the awful things that could happen to Kyrion and me in the real world if we didn't figure out the nuances of our bond.

Those ominous butterflies dropped and congealed into bricks of dread lining my stomach. I didn't know what was going on, but I needed to get past the fire-spewing cauldron.

I grabbed more orange pebbles and eased along the safe side of the path. The trees crowded up to the edge of the flagstones, and I peered into the shrubbery, searching for more traps.

Click.

A flagstone depressed under my feet, and a low gray vine lashed out and slapped against my right ankle like a whip. I tripped and went down hard on all fours, and pain exploded in my hands and knees. I cursed, but before I could scramble to my feet, the vine lashed out again and coiled around my ankle like a heavy rope anchoring me to the ground.

Not a natural vine but a mechanical one painted to blend in with the rest of the shrubbery. Clever. I reached for the vine, but it tightened like a vise—and then it jerked forward and started dragging me along the ground.

I yelped in surprise and tried to grab one of the flagstones to stop the unwanted movement, but they were all smooth and slick, and I couldn't get a grip on any of them. Digging my boots into the ground didn't help much either, since the machinery was a lot stronger than I was. Slowly but surely, the vine pulled me back onto the left path and headed straight toward the metal nozzle of the fire trap.

Worry squeezed my heart, but I forced myself to push it aside. I reached for my seer power and studied everything around me, from the ground to the flagstones to the charred petals still drifting through the air. I needed something to help disable the vine or at least force it to release its grip, or I was about to be extra crispy.

A pale silver glow appeared near the hibiscus trees the fire trap had decimated. I peered in that direction and reached for even more of my magic, and the glow solidified on a fallen branch that had smashed one of the lizard statues along the path. My gaze locked onto the lizard's tail, which had broken off into a large, long shard with a sharp, daggerlike edge. Just like the rock in my pocket, it wasn't much of a weapon, but it would have to do.

I quit fighting the vine's insistent pull. Instead, I lay down on my left hip and curved my left arm out to the side. I waited until the machinery had dragged me as close to the smashed statue as possible, then dug my boots into the ground, surged forward, and stretched my hand out as far as it would go, reaching, reaching, reaching for the lizard's tail . . .

My fingers brushed against the broken stone, but I couldn't quite grab it. The vine yanked at me like I was a dog on a leash. I resisted its movement as much as possible, but it was a losing battle. Twenty more seconds, and the vine would pull me directly into the fire nozzle trap, so I growled and stretched out a little further . . . and a little further still . . .

My fingers closed around the stone. The sharp edge nicked my skin, making me hiss, but I ignored the slice of pain and yanked the shard toward me. The instant I had a good grip on the lizard's tail, I sat up and dug my boots into the ground, fighting the vine's relentless pull as much as possible. Then I leaned forward, shoved the shard up against the vine, and started sawing away with the sharp edge of the lizard's tail.

The machinery sputtered, but it didn't stop, so I kept sawing . . . and sawing . . . and sawing . . .

Lucky for me, the vine had been built for flexibility and movement, instead of armored strength, and the broken stone sheared through the plastic casing, exposing the wiring underneath. I growled and redoubled my efforts, using the shard to cut through the wiring. Sparks flew out, stinging my hands, but once again, I kept sawing . . . and sawing . . . and sawing . . .

Beep!

With a sad little wail, the wiring snapped, and the vine finally stilled.

I wiped the clammy sweat off my forehead with a shaking hand, then quickly uncoiled the machinery from around my ankle and scrambled to my feet. The lizard's tail slipped out of my hand and crunched under my boots like a broken bone.

I grimaced and scanned the biodome, looking for more vines and nozzles, but none appeared. Even more wary than before, I gathered up a handful of orange pebbles and returned to the right, safe path. I stopped every few feet and tossed another pebble out onto the flagstones in front of me, but I didn't trigger any more traps.

I made it around the cauldron safely and stepped across another threshold, moving from the warm Tropics biodome back into the chilly maze. I exhaled and wiped a bit more sweat off my forehead. No wonder warriors found the maze so challenging. If the first, obvious obstacle didn't get you, then a second, hidden one would.

I stopped and called out with the bond again. *Kyrion? Can you hear me?*

No response, although the sticky cobweb of him in my mind once again bristled with tension. A few more bricks of worry landed in my stomach. What challenges was Kyrion facing on his side of the maze?

I moved forward. More nozzles jutted out of the metal walls and spewed fog into the air. The clouds weren't nearly as thick as they had been in the first section, but the hazy white mist still made it seem like I was traveling through a strange dreamscape.

I grabbed hold of the bond, letting my connection to Kyrion guide me forward. I went down one path after another, moving deeper and deeper into the maze. Several paths were dead ends, forcing me to backtrack time and time again, but I got the sense that I was slowly drawing closer to Kyrion.

Magnets, just like Lady Verona had said.

A few minutes later, I came to a biodome that contained an elegant topiary garden that reminded me of those on the Collier estate. Gray-green trees and hedges snipped into the shapes of lighthouses, anchors, and spiral seashells clustered around white marble statues of mermaids wearing gold necklaces strung with gleaming white, gray, and black pearls that were as big as my fist. In the center of the dome, a mermaid brandished a silver trident at a tall, wide hedge that had been sculpted into an enormous jellyfish, complete with long, dangling tendrils.

I stepped over the threshold and let out a sigh of relief. The air in the biodome matched a warm spring day on a Temperate planet.

I studied the topiary trees and hedges, along with the statues, but I didn't spot any trip wires, fire nozzles, or mechanical vines. I glanced down at the flagstones, but they were smooth and whole and didn't show any signs of tampering. I even stretched out with my seer magic, but no telltale silver flares of light appeared, indicating useful or dangerous objects.

Hmm. Maybe the lack of traps was the trap itself, to cost

me precious time I could be using to reach the center of the maze.

Still wary, I eased forward, but nothing happened. No fog, no flames, no other elements appeared. My steps quickened, and I hurried along a path, skirting around the jellyfish topiary.

I reached out with the bond again, but Kyrion didn't seem any closer. Frustration filled me, but I kept moving forward—

Clank.

I froze at the sharp sound. I glanced around, but the flag-stones remained still and solid beneath my boots, and I hadn't stumbled over a trip wire or brushed up against a topiary. I hadn't activated a trap, so what had made that odd noise?

Clank. Clank-clank. Clank.

More sharp sounds boomed out like ominous thunder that was loud enough to vibrate the energy shield overhead. My stomach clenched. Why did that noise seem so familiar?

Off to my left, two bright neon-green glows flared to life. I whirled in that direction, careful not to step on another flag-stone or venture off the path.

Branches creaked and cracked, and the long tendrils on the jellyfish topiary swayed back and forth, like it was a real creature floating through the ocean. More branches creaked and cracked, and a large figure tore through the topiary like a monster breaking free of a cage. Green eyes, black armor, hulking frame—it was another Black Scarab.

The Black Scarab stopped. Its arms and legs twisted back and forth, and its head spun all the way around on its wide shoulders, sending a violent shower of leaves into the air.

A breath hissed out between my teeth. This Scarab looked even more lifelike than the hologram I'd seen earlier, and the explosion of leaves was a nice added touch to make it seem even more real and substantial.

The Scarab took a step forward.

Clank.

The flagstone cracked under the weight of the Scarab's heavy armor. The machine took another step forward, resulting in another *clank* and cracked flagstone.

Shock knifed through my heart. This wasn't a hologram. This was a very real, very dangerous Black Scarab, and its green gaze was locked on me.

SEVEN

KYRION

Instead of immediately moving forward along the entry path, I held my position, adjusting to the sight, scent, sound, and feel of the maze.

The green vines were packed so tightly together that not much of the metal walls could be seen between or behind them, and the honeysuckles' sweet aroma was strong enough to make my nose twitch. The gray stone path was solid and sturdy beneath my boots, but a hint of a breeze slid across my body from the dome's ventilation system. The air itself was surprisingly cool, and my breath steamed in faint clouds of frost. The overhead lights had been turned down low, creating large pools of shadows.

I reached for my power and waggled my fingers. My telekinesis came to me easily, and a few fallen pink petals skittered away from my boots.

Next, I reached for the truebond. My connection to Vesper felt thin and distant, as though our bond had completely unspooled and I was just barely touching the end of the velvety ribbon of her presence in my mind. My inner monster grumbled in annoyance.

The hidden psionic dampeners weren't affecting my innate abilities, but they shrouded the maze like a heavy, invisible blanket and were clearly muffling our connection. Trying to break through the dampeners to locate and communicate with Vesper was going to be more difficult than I'd expected, but testing our bond was the reason we'd come here.

Overhead, a camera zipped down from the ceiling and swiveled toward me. Red lights burned on the front of the camera, and the lens inside twisted open, then closed, like it was a gaping black eye. More annoyance filled me. I didn't know which was worse, the camera tracking my movements or the holocuff clamped around my left wrist recording my every breath, blink, and twitch.

My hand clenched over the empty spot where my stormsword would normally be hooked to my belt. I'd worn the weapon for so many years that it was practically an extension of my hand, and I felt weak, naked, and clumsy without it. Earlier in the locker room, I'd thought about tucking a dagger from my silver bandolier up my jacket sleeve and sneaking the weapon into the maze, but I'd decided against it. Cheating was for insecure people who had no true confidence in their own abilities, and I wanted to complete the training fair and square. Otherwise, it wouldn't *mean* anything.

The camera lens kept twisting open and closed as it zoomed in and out. I gave an elegant bow to Asterin, Siya, Jeffrey, and whoever else might be watching. Then I headed deeper into the maze.

I moved cautiously, scanning the walls on either side of the path as well as the flagstones up ahead for any unusual glints of metal or thick seams that would indicate hidden mechanisms. But I didn't spot anything unexpected, and I quickly came to a junction that split left and right.

Each path looked the same, and I couldn't tell which direction might get me closer to the center of the maze. Since I didn't have any visual cues, I once again reached for the bond.

Vesper?

She didn't respond to my telepathic call, but the velvety ribbon of her in my mind quivered, like she was thinking about something. No doubt she was dealing with her own obstacles on her side of the maze.

I concentrated on our connection, but I couldn't tell if I was any closer to Vesper, so I would just have to guess which path to take. I huffed out a breath. I *despised* guessing games. There was no skill or thought involved, just dumb, blind luck, which had never been kind to me.

I stepped onto the path that curved to the right. A hundred feet later, this path also split. One section continued to curve along the exterior of the maze, while the other section veered into the interior at a sharp angle. I wasn't going to find Vesper by sticking to the perimeter, so I chose the path that led deeper into the labyrinth.

The path snaked around before opening into a circular area that was several hundred feet wide and covered by a clear, shimmering energy shield that extended all the way down to the ground. On the other side of the shield, the honeysuckle vines vanished, replaced by smooth metal walls covered with a thick layer of glittering blue-white frost. At least two feet of snow coated the ground in a sparkling sheen, while pellets of ice zipped through the air, propelled by a man-made wind.

This biodome had been fashioned after the harsh environment of a Frozon moon, and it resembled a life-size snow globe.

The only things that weren't cold and frozen were the flagstone paths that arced around a large stone fountain shaped like a castle in the center of the biodome. Water bubbled and frothed in a steady stream down the castle's many towers and walls before pooling in the fountain's wide basin. Red flags bearing the black *B* sigil of House Battis topped the castle's towers, and the stiff swatches of fabric stood out like blood drops against the snow-white background. The fountain was probably a miniature version of the real Castle Battis.

I huffed out another annoyed breath. Out of all the biodomes, I'd come across the coldest environment, and there was no way I could get through the area unscathed. At the very least, I would be chilled to the bone. At the very worst, I might suffer severe frostbite. Once again, luck was not being kind to me.

For a moment, I considered backtracking, but that would take an inordinate amount of time. No, it was better to brave this biodome, continue deeper into the maze, and find Vesper as quickly as possible.

First, I buttoned my jacket up to my neck and pulled my sleeves down as far as they would go. Next, I shoved my hands into my armpits to protect my fingers from the cold. Finally, I drew in a breath, steeled myself for what was coming next, and plunged through the energy shield.

As soon as I entered the Frozon biodome, pellets of ice gusted through the air even more violently, like I had stepped into the middle of a raging blizzard. A couple of fist-size pellets slammed into my legs, and I had to brace my boots against the flagstones to keep from getting knocked off the path into a snowdrift. My face went numb, and the air was so sharp and cold I felt like I was breathing in jagged icicles.

The flagstones must have been heated, because they were free of the ice and snow that coated the rest of the ground. I hurried along the path until I reached the fountain. It too must have been heated, because the water kept tumbling down at a steady rate before pooling in the basin, getting sucked back up to the top, and falling right back down again.

The path split left and right, circling around the fountain. Once again, each path looked the same, and I had to make a quick, blind choice or risk becoming even colder—

Clank.

An odd, muffled noise whispered through the air, freezing me in place. It wasn't blaster fire, which I had heard a thousand times before and would immediately put me on high alert, but something about the noise was oddly familiar and extremely troubling.

I tilted my head to the side, listening, but the noise didn't come again, and all I heard was the whistle of the manufactured wind in the biodome. Perhaps it had just been some hidden machinery activating in the snow. Either way, I needed to get out of the Frozon environment as quickly as possible, so I stepped onto the right path and headed around the fountain.

Click!

A flagstone depressed under my boot, and a tiny glass window on one of the castle's towers flipped down. A metal nozzle jutted out of the opening and shot out a spray of water that zipped straight toward my chest.

I whipped in that direction, snapped up my right hand, and used my telekinesis to send the water away from my body.

Click!

Even though I didn't step onto another flagstone and trip another trap, another window on the castle fountain flipped down, and a second nozzle appeared, shooting water at me from a different angle. I spun to the side and punched my arms out in opposite directions, using my telekinesis to force both sprays of water away from my body.

The water pressure was dialed up to maximum capacity, and the hard, bruising jets slammed against my telekinesis, inching closer and closer to my body. Even more alarming was the fact that the sprays of liquid that hit the ground sizzled and melted through the crusty snow, as though the water had been mixed with a corrosive acid.

I ground my teeth, braced my feet, and gripped my power even more tightly. I couldn't afford to let a single drop of water touch my skin. The wetness would only exacerbate the potential for frostbite and hypothermia, while the acid would burn my skin the same way it was eating through the snow.

Cold sweat prickled my forehead from the effort of using so much of my psion power to redirect the water, but I didn't dare break my concentration to lift an arm and wipe the freezing dampness away. My focus narrowed to those two jets of water, which kept blasting against my telekinesis.

One second after another ticked by, and the water just kept coming and coming. How much liquid was in this bloody fountain?

Suddenly, the two jets of water sputtered once, twice, three times before the streams died down into a series of drips that quickly froze into a trail of icicles hanging down from the nozzles.

I kept my arms raised, just in case it was a trick to get me to lower my guard so the water could restart. But nothing happened, and after about fifteen seconds, I finally dropped my arms, released my grip on my telekinesis, and hissed out a tense breath.

I silently cursed my own foolishness. I'd been so distracted by the snow and ice and so determined to get out of the Frozon biodome as quickly as possible that I hadn't bothered to scan the path for traps. If I'd been in a Techwave facility, I would have been blasted with cannon fire instead of water, and I would have been dead. Or worse, some bounty hunters could have knocked me unconscious, trussed me up like a solstice ham, and shipped me back to Callus Holloway. I couldn't afford to make such a stupid, sloppy mistake in the real world. Not if I wanted to keep Vesper safe.

Despite the biting wind whistling across my body and the pellets of ice once again stinging my face, I held my position for several more seconds, until the two nozzles had completely iced over.

When I was certain the water trap had been played out, I shoved my hands back into my armpits, trying to bring as much warmth as possible to my chilled fingers. Next, I glanced down and studied the flagstone beneath my boots. I had to squint through the cascade of ice pellets, but I spotted a small drop of water carved into the top-left corner.

I studied the other flagstones ahead. A few more stones had the telltale water drop carved into their left corners, but most were smooth and blank. I hesitated, wondering if the answer was that simple, but my body was numb, and I couldn't afford to stay in the Frozon biodome any longer. Even though the water trap hadn't touched me, the resulting dampness had made the air even more frigid.

I drew in a breath, shifted my weight into my toes, and hopped onto the closest unmarked flagstone.

My boots thumped against the stone. I tensed and kept a wary eye on the fountain, but no more castle windows opened, and no more nozzles appeared. I exhaled and moved on.

I skipped, hopped, and jumped from one safe stone to the next like I was playing a child's game. On the backside of the fountain, the path straightened, and I quickly strode through the energy shield that cordoned off the Frozon biodome.

After the frigid snowscape, the cool air in the maze was as warm as a sauna. I jumped up and down, shook out my arms and legs, flexed my fingers and toes, wrinkled my nose, and slapped my cheeks several times. The numbness that gripped my body slowly faded away, replaced by a welcome, if painful, tingling. My skin was dry, tight, and chapped, but I hadn't suffered any major, lasting damage from the extreme cold.

I exhaled with relief, then hurried on.

A few hundred feet later, I came to a large junction where the path split off in five directions. Once again, all the paths looked the same, and I had no idea which way to go. I reached out with the bond, hoping to use it to plot a course forward, but Vesper didn't seem any closer, despite how deep I was in the maze.

A frustrated growl rose in my throat, but I closed my eyes and reached for the bond again. This time, I focused solely on the velvety ribbon of Vesper in my mind. Her presence still felt faint and far away, so I concentrated on gripping the ribbon and then slowly moving along it, like I was putting one hand in front of the other and climbing along a horizontal rope. The ribbon vibrated with tension, and I turned my head, following the motion . . .

The velvety ribbon of Vesper stilled. I opened my eyes and found myself looking down a path that led to the left. I shook my arms and legs out a final time, getting rid of the last of the tingling, then strode in that direction.

Clank. Clank-clank. Clank.

I stopped. What was that? No more noises sounded, but dread pooled in my gut. I knew those odd sounds, even if I couldn't remember exactly what they were right now.

Wary, I eased forward, once again scanning the walls around me, as well as the path ahead. I didn't see any traps, and I quickly made it to another junction, where the maze once again split in five directions. I hesitated, unsure of which path to take—

Shock punched into my chest as though someone had just stabbed me with a stormsword. The sharp, unexpected emotion threw me off-balance, and I staggered to the right.

Click.

A flagstone depressed under my boot, and a silver nozzle jutted out of the honeysuckle vines to my left. On instinct, I threw myself forward and down onto the path.

Pew! Pew! Pew!

Blaster bolts shot out of a weapon hidden in the wall. The

bright orange streaks sliced through the air at chest height and slammed into the vines on the opposite side of the path. Smoke and sparks boiled up into the air in an acrid cloud.

Several seconds ticked by. No more bolts shot out, so I lifted my head and climbed back up to my feet. Careful not to trigger another trap, I went over and plucked a honeysuckle blossom off one of the damaged vines. The blackened, brittle petals crumbled to ash in my hand.

Given the minor burns I'd seen on the House Battis Hammers in the locker room, I had assumed the blasters and other weapons in the maze would be set to stun, just as they had been for the other warriors. But the scorched vines and acrid smoke still billowing into the air indicated this weapon had more than enough juice to inflict a serious injury, maybe even a mortal one, if I was unlucky enough to get hit in just the wrong spot.

Puzzlement filled me. Why change the intensity of the weapons for me and Vesper? Was this part of Lord Aldrich and Lady Verona's truebond training program? But why would the Colliers risk us being so badly hurt? It simply didn't make any sense.

I dusted the ash off my hand, even more wariness flickering through me—

Another sword of shock stabbed into my chest. This time, I was able to maintain my balance, although my heart started pounding with worry.

Vesper? I called out with my telepathy. *Vesper!*

I didn't receive a thought in return, but the velvety ribbon of her vibrated like a viper warning of danger.

Something was wrong.

EIGHT

VESPER

I remained frozen in place, gaping at the Black Scarab, one question after another spinning through my mind.

How had a real Black Scarab gotten into the training facility? Much less all the way into the depths of the maze? Was this the only machine? Or were more automated troops invading the area at this very moment?

That last, terrifying thought finally penetrated my shock, and I looked past the Scarab, searching the biodome for more enemies.

In my experience, Black Scarabs almost always had a human minder or two to control the machines and tell them who, what, when, where, and how to attack. I tilted my head to the side and listened. No more clanking footsteps rang out, and I didn't hear any shouts that would indicate human Techwave soldiers were nearby.

I frowned. If no Techwave soldiers had breached the facility, then someone from House Battis must have placed the Black Scarab in the maze. Why? Was the automated troop part of the truebond training program? Did Siya and Asterin know about the machine? And how could someone from House Battis have possibly gotten their hands on a Scarab in the first place? General Orion Ocnus, one of the Techwave leaders, didn't just lend out his toy soldiers like a kid swapping playing cards of their favorite athletes.

More questions whirred through my mind, but how and why the Black Scarab had gotten here didn't really matter. No, the only thing that mattered right now was the fact that my only weapon was the chunk of rock still tucked in my pocket.

Vesper? Vesper! Kyrion's voice sounded in my mind, but his tone was weak and raspy, like it was taking every ounce of his strength and telepathy to overcome the psionic dampeners and send a thought to me.

Kyrion! There's a Black Scarab in the maze!

I waited, but he didn't respond. At least, not with words. The sticky cobweb of Kyrion bristled with worry, but I couldn't tell if the emotion was for me or if he had run into a Black Scarab on his side of the maze.

My stomach clenched with dread at the idea of Kyrion facing one of the mechanized troops without any weapons, but I pushed the emotion aside. Kyrion wasn't here, and I needed to worry about myself right now.

Clank.

The Scarab took another slow, lumbering step forward, then jerked to a halt. Gears ground together deep inside the machine, and its green eyes widened and brightened at the same time.

A fresh wave of dread crashed over me, although it quickly receded, replaced by more questions. Why let me see the Scarab at all? Why not let me walk by the topiary trap, then have the machine come up behind me and squish my skull like a grape? What—or who—was the Scarab waiting for?

Click-click.

I tensed, but the Scarab didn't move, and the noises sounded like they had come from . . . above. I glanced up. The camera that had been trailing me through the maze had dropped down through the energy shield that covered the garden biodome and was now only about thirty feet above my head. The camera was also right above the Black Scarab, as though whoever was controlling the camera was also using it to control the mechanized troop.

I stared up into the lens, which widened, just like the Scarab's eyes had. Okay, that was creepy. But the strangest thing was the *feeling* emanating from the camera—a giddy mix of glee and anticipation, like the real fun was about to begin.

I shivered. Kyrion's telempathy was the most unpredictable of his powers, and it usually only let me sense strong emotions from other people. The fact that it had surged now, despite the psionic dampeners blocking our connection, indicated just how excited my watcher was to see me battle the Black Scarab. This might have started as a training exercise, but something else was going on now, something that was much more dangerous than eerie clouds of fog, subtle trip wires, jets of fire, and mechanical vines.

The lens widened a little more. Maybe it was a quirk of my seer magic, but for a moment, I saw my own reflection in the glass, along with Kyrion's worried face.

Clank-clank.

The Black Scarab stepped forward, then stretched out with its left hand, like it was merely trying to grab my arm instead of ripping the limb off the rest of my body. I spun to the side, moving past the machine's outstretched hand and keeping clear of its thick, strong fingers.

The Scarab whirled around, as did the overhead camera. The machine jerked forward and made another slow, lumbering swipe, like it was still intent on merely capturing instead of killing me. Weird. I dodged this new attack, then backed away from the Scarab, my mind dreaming up and discarding one desperate plan after another.

First things first. If my unwanted watcher was using the overhead camera to control the Scarab, then maybe getting rid of the device would stop the machine in its tracks—or at least make it more difficult for my enemy to see my every movement.

I yanked the rock I'd picked up earlier out of my pocket and hefted it in my hand, getting a feel for its shape, size, and weight. The rock was heavy, and I didn't have the necessary strength to get it where I needed it to go, but Kyrion did—if I could use his telekinesis.

Doubt curled through my stomach, but I brushed it aside. I didn't have time for doubt right now, only rogue actions that would keep me alive and out of the Scarab's clutches.

I looked up at the camera again and snapped off a mock salute with my left hand. "You wanted my attention?" I called out. "Well, you got it."

I drew my right arm back and hurled the rock at the camera. As soon as the chunk of stone left my hand, I reached for Kyrion's telekinesis. Once again, I became lost in that mental haze, searching blindly for something I knew was there but couldn't quite see through the white fog wisping through my mind. I ground my teeth, ignored the cool, distracting mist, and plunged my hand directly into the sticky cobweb of Kyrion.

Touching his presence was like closing my fingers around a live wire. My heart jolted, my skin sizzled, and white-hot stars exploded in my field of vision. The jolting, sizzling sensations vanished just as quickly as they had appeared, and the stars winked out, replaced by the creeping white fog, which threatened to muffle our connection once again.

I tightened my grip on that sticky cobweb, letting all those tiny strands anchor me to Kyrion. The creeping fog in my mind stopped, and Kyrion's power trickled toward me like water seeping through hairline cracks in a dam. I latched onto that power and gathered up as much of his telekinesis as I could.

Then I sent all that magic shooting up and out at the rock I'd thrown, making the chunk of stone rise higher and higher until . . .

Crack!

The rock smashed into the camera and sheared the device off its long black wire. The rock plummeted downward, along with the camera, and I had to lurch out of the way to keep from being bonked on the head by the falling debris.

The camera landed a few feet away and bounced across a couple of flagstones before spinning to a stop. The red lights on the device flashed a few times, then winked out.

My gaze darted over to the Scarab, but it didn't move. My heart lifted. I'd done it. I'd disabled the machine—

Clank-clank.

The Black Scarab jerked forward. My heart plummeted. Disabling the camera hadn't stopped the machine.

The Scarab's head spun around on its shoulders, and its neon-green eyes locked onto me. The machine's hands clenched into fists, and it sprinted toward me.

NINE

KYRION

The velvety ribbon of Vesper continued to whip around in my mind, matching the arrows of worry streaking through my gut. Forget the training exercise. Something was wrong, and I needed to find Vesper.

I spun around and stepped forward. I needed to backtrack to the entrance and get out of the maze as quickly as possible.

Bang!

A metal wall shot out, blocking the path and making me stop short. What had just happened?

My shock vanished, and my inner monster roared with rage. I slammed my fist against the wall, but of course, the metal didn't give or move.

Bang! Bang! Bang!

One by one, more metal walls shot out and slammed into place, blocking four of the five paths. My inner monster roared again, and an answering growl rumbled through my chest. Whoever was controlling the maze had left me with only one path, forcing me in the direction they wanted.

Why? What had changed? What in all the bloody stars was going on?

"All right, all right," I muttered. "You win—for now."

Overhead, the camera that had been trailing me through the maze dropped a little lower and shifted up and down, almost as if it was nodding in approval. I glared up at the camera, and for a moment, I could have sworn I saw my reflection in the lens, along with Vesper's, as though we were both looking straight into the device at the same time, even though that was impossible.

Vesper? I called out with my telepathy.

She didn't answer, but the velvety ribbon of her hummed with satisfaction, like she had just figured out a difficult problem. Relief swept through me, and I stood there, drinking in Vesper's warm, strong, solid presence in my mind. And she was going to stay that way, I vowed. No matter what I had to do—or whom I had to kill—to get out of here.

I glared up at the camera again. "You want me to go somewhere?" I called out in a mocking voice. "Then show me the way."

The camera didn't move this time, but the lens opened a little wider. Disgust curled through me. No answers there.

I had no choice but to step onto the only open path. I moved as quickly as I dared, still leery of traps, but I didn't see any nozzles or other hazards hidden in the honeysuckle vines. The lack of obstacles made me even more wary. The previous sections of the maze had been a warm-up, and now I was headed straight for the main event—whatever it was.

A few minutes later, I came to a junction. Once again, metal walls shot out, blocking two of the three paths.

"To the right it is," I muttered, and moved in that direction.

I strode along one path after another. Every time I came to a junction, more walls appeared, forcing me onto the sole remaining path and shepherding me onward.

A couple of minutes later, my current forced path opened into an enormous circle that was even larger than the Frozon biodome I'd blundered through earlier. No energy shield covered this biodome, so it was the same temperature as the rest of the maze. The area looked like a common garden, although the honeysuckle vines were only waist high and mixed with blue-moon peonies and other flowers. I eyed the blossoms, all of which were much larger and more colorful than usual, almost as if they were given a special fertilizer to make them grow to their fullest potential. How strange.

A couple of fountains bubbled around the perimeter, right next to several black marble statues shaped like the same House Battis castle I'd seen in the Frozon biodome. Several paths branched off the garden, but they were all sealed off by metal walls.

My gaze locked onto the lone figure standing in the center of the garden. Shiny red plates of polyplastic armor covered the figure's arms and legs, while heavy black boots with red armored tips encased their feet. A matching breastplate boasting the large *B* of House Battis stretched across the figure's chest, and the sigil glimmered brightly, like it was made of metallic black ink that had been stamped into the red polyplastic.

All put together, the figure looked like a scaled-down, humanoid version of a Black Scarab. For a moment, I thought it was a hologram, but then I noticed the figure's familiar features—dark brown hair and eyes, tan skin, square jaw.

Roderick Battis grinned, his white teeth glinting in his chiseled face. "Hello, Kyrion," he crooned. "I've been waiting for you."

I blinked and blinked, but my vision remained sharp and clear. Roderick Battis was standing in front of me clad in a bloodred, human version of Black Scarab armor. But it wasn't just standard armor. A large holoscreen was embedded in the polyplastic on his left forearm, and the plates molded to his arms, chest, and legs like a second skin, as though the armor had been custom-made for him.

My gaze skipped over to the weapon dangling from his right hand. Roderick might be wearing Scarab armor, but he was clutching a traditional Erzton war hammer. He swung the hammer back and forth, and the opalescent lunarium glimmered with a pale red light in a reflection of his psion power.

"I'm so happy you're finally here," Roderick crooned again.

"Why in all the stars would you be happy I'm here?"

Roderick held his arms out wide, like the answer should be obvious. "Because you're Kyrion Caldaren, the former head of the Imperium Arrows and one of the most feared and notorious warriors in the Archipelago Galaxy. You've survived more battles and engaged in more rogue actions in the last few months than a legion of Hammers do in their entire lives. It's impressive. *You're* impressive. I truly mean that."

"What's your point?" I snapped.

Roderick's eyes gleamed with a dark, sinister light, and a strange, nauseating eagerness wafted off him and twinged my telempathy. "My point is simple—that you, Kyrion Caldaren, are the best of the best, and I'm going to relish testing myself against you."

Roderick was chattering away like this was still a training exercise, but I'd walked into enough bad situations over the years to realize exactly how much danger I was in. Vesper too, since she was also in the maze.

Vesper? I called out with my telepathy. *Vesper!*

She didn't respond, but the velvety ribbon of her in my mind rippled with determination. Relief shot through me, but it was quickly followed by worry. If Roderick was here, then who—or what—had he sent after Vesper?

Roderick kept staring at me, that smug, stupid grin still plastered across his face like it was his birthday and I was his new favorite toy. Anger boiled in my gut, but I tamped it down. I needed to keep Roderick talking and learn exactly what he was plotting. Then I could figure out some way to kill him and find Vesper.

"Why would you want to test yourself against me?" I asked.

"Thanks to the major Erzton Houses desperately clinging to their neutral stances, all we Hammers do is train and train and train some more. Everyone knows the Techwave wants to topple the Erzton just as badly as they want to crush the Imperium, but none of the Erzton Houses can agree on a course of action. Indecisive cowards." Disgust colored Roderick's voice, and his lips curled back into a derisive sneer.

He shook his head and swept his war hammer out wide, encompassing the entire dome. "Did you know that this used to be an arena? And not just any arena but the finest one in all the Erzton. Hammers from Houses throughout the galaxy would come here and compete in tournaments."

His eyes softened with memories, and he cocked his head to the side, as though he could hear the raucous cheers of long-ago crowds.

Roderick's gaze cleared, and his lips curled back into another sneer. "Now Hammers from rival Houses can't even have a minor skirmish without it turning into a galactic *incident*."

A chilling realization swept through me, and I started to see the sharp edges of his elaborate trap. "So you decided to recreate that arena and those glory days."

"Of course!" Roderick twirled his hammer around, once again encompassing the entire dome. "My House built the finest training facility credits can buy. It's only fitting I use my arena to its fullest potential."

You simply must *come on my next hunt. We're going to Frozon 15. Several packs of wolves and bears can be found on the moon, as well as some ice dragons and wyverns . . . They should provide me with a decent challenge, for a change.* Roderick's earlier words to Asterin whispered through my mind.

"Why? Did hunting Frozon wolves and Tropics tigers become too boring and passé?" I sniped.

Roderick chuckled. "Hunting animals is all well and good, but in the end, that's all they are—*animals*. You track them, trap them, and then you kill them and the game is over." His lips split into a thin smile. "So a few years ago, I decided to create my own game and stock it with much more interesting prey."

Twin fists of disgust and anger punched into my chest. "People," I growled. "You're hunting *people*."

"Not just people," Roderick corrected. "The finest warriors in the galaxy. Erzton, Imperium, Techwave, I don't discriminate."

His dark gaze trailed down my body, and a thoughtful look filled the lord's face, as though I was a side of beef he was inspecting for his dinner table. "Although I've never had the chance to test my skills against an Arrow before. Well, former Arrow. But let's not quibble about titles and semantics."

"Oh, no," I snarked. "We wouldn't want to do something as gauche as that."

Roderick started pacing back and forth and swinging his hammer from side to side. Once again, the lunarium shimmered a pale red in a reflection of his power, which scraped against my telempathy like a piece of sandpaper. The Erzton lord was a strong psion, which made him a dangerous enemy, and his polyplastic armor and lunarium war hammer gave him a huge advantage.

"I'll admit that I was surprised when I was first approached about asking you and Vesper to train here," Roderick said. "But then I realized the opportunity was too good to pass up."

"What *opportunity*?" I growled again.

A smug smile stretched across his face. "An opportunity to

test my skills not only against an Arrow but against one who has the added power of a truebond. You truly are a remarkable creature, Kyrion. One of a kind. Even rarer than a red Tropics tiger or a blue Frozon wolf."

I wasn't one of a kind. I was a bond of two, tried and true. I was the cold blue moon to Vesper's white-hot star, as Lady Verona had once said, and right now I was much more worried for my partner than I was for myself.

"Where's Vesper?" I demanded. "What have you done to her?"

"Vesper is a seer, not a psion like you, Kyrion," Roderick scoffed. "She's hardly worth the effort it would take to hunt her down, so I let Jeffrey handle her. He had a new toy he wanted to test out on her."

My hands clenched into fists, and it took every ounce of my self-control not to lunge forward, wrap my hands around the bastard's throat, and choke the answers out of him. "What sort of *toy*?"

Roderick shrugged. "Jeffrey was recently gifted a Black Scarab by some new friends of mine. He plugged it into the maze control panel last week. He's still working out a few bugs in the system, and he's just been *dying* to test it out on someone new."

Ice rushed through my veins. Vesper was trapped in the maze with a Black Scarab and no stormsword to defend herself. I thought of the shock that had stabbed into my chest earlier. That must have been Vesper coming face-to-face with the Scarab.

Vesper? Vesper! I called out through the bond.

She didn't answer, but the velvety ribbon of her in my mind was still warm, strong, and firm. Whatever had happened, the Scarab hadn't hurt Vesper, which eased some of my worry. Still, I needed to get to her as quickly as possible, which meant getting past Roderick.

"So you got Jeffrey to force me into this garden so you could do what, exactly? Fight me?" I shook my head. "That won't end so well for you. Trust me on that."

Roderick arched an eyebrow. "Why? Because you have the storied power of a truebond and I don't? Truebonds are highly overrated, Kyrion. Trust me on that."

A knowing smirk stretched across his face, and a sickening realization knifed through my gut. "You lured another truebond couple into the maze."

Roderick nodded. "Unfortunately, one of the maze technicians discovered what I was doing in the facility after hours. Jason threatened to go to the gossipcasts unless I bought his silence."

"What did you do to him?"

"I told Jason to meet me here so I could transfer the credits to his account. Jason was foolish enough to leave Caleb, his younger brother and truebonded partner, alone at their apartment. As soon as Jason left to meet me, a few of my trusted Hammers stormed the apartment, captured Caleb, and brought him here. I told Jason what I'd done, and he rushed into the maze to try to save his brother. But it was too late, and Jeffrey's Black Scarab had already torn poor Caleb to pieces." Roderick clucked his tongue in mock sympathy.

More ice rushed through my veins. I hadn't known Jason and Caleb, but I knew what a broken bond could do to the remaining partner. My father had gone mad with grief over the loss of his connection to my mother. So had Adria Byrne, an Arrow who'd been bonded to her brother, Dargan, when Vesper killed him during the Regal midnight ball. Oh, yes. A severed truebond usually wreaked utter devastation that very few people could survive.

Roderick's lips puckered in thought. "Looking back, I really should have battled Jason first. He was by far the superior warrior, but after Caleb was killed, Jason didn't put up a fight at all. He just held Caleb's body, rocked back and forth, and sobbed. At least, until I broke his jaw with my hammer to shut him up."

Roderick shrugged again, as though deliberately luring two people into his maze for the sole purpose of killing them was of no more consequence than playing a video game. That's exactly what this was to Roderick, a bloody *game*. Only he didn't even have the decency to play fair, given his armor and war hammer. No, Roderick Battis only wanted to play if he was certain he could win. Fucking coward.

"You want to fight an Arrow?" I jerked my chin toward his chest. "Then take off the armor and drop the hammer, and we'll see who the better warrior truly is."

"Nah," Roderick replied. "I was smart enough to lure you into my hunting ground. That already makes me the better warrior, Kyrion. But I'll be happy to prove it to you."

He lifted the holoscreen on his left forearm to his lips. "Open the gates and disable the traps in section forty-seven."

Several soft whirs sounded. Around the biodome, the metal walls slid back, revealing the various paths.

Roderick lowered his arm and looked at me. Once again, that strange, disgusting eagerness wafted off him and twinged my telempathy. "You have a choice, Kyrion. You can stay here and fight me, or you can go back into the maze and try to find Vesper—"

I whirled around and sprinted back in the direction I'd come from. Roderick might have ordered Jeffrey to disable the traps, but I didn't trust him. Right now, the safest, quickest path was the one I'd already explored, if only because I'd al-ready seen the dangers on it.

Behind me, a bark of delighted laughter rang out, along with Roderick's loud, thumping footsteps. He might have called it a choice, but really, he had just given me a head start to prolong his twisted hunt. Roderick had snapped the jaws of his trap shut, and now he wanted to see how long and how violently I would thrash around.

I quickened my pace. Let him laugh and chase after me.

All that mattered was finding Vesper before it was too late.

TEN

VESPER

The Black Scarab sprinted toward me and lowered its shoulder like it wanted to ram into me like a player in a sports game. If that happened, I wouldn't be getting back up again anytime soon.

I dove to the side. My left shoulder slammed into a flagstone, and pain exploded in the joint. I grunted at the hard, bruising impact, but I forced myself to scramble back up and onto my feet.

The Black Scarab raced past me and plowed into one of the topiary trees. Branches snapped, and leaves twirled through the air like gray-green snowflakes. The machine jerked back, but it had plunged into the very center of the tree, and it was caught like a butterfly in a net. Hope sparked in my heart, but the Scarab jerked back again, and several branches cracked away. I had a minute, maybe less, before the machine freed itself.

I could leave the Temperate garden biodome and sprint down a path, but I couldn't outrun the Scarab. I also didn't know what traps I might trip along the way or how many more Scarabs might be lurking in the maze.

Once again, I was stuck in the middle of an OBO—a situation where I had only bad options.

My chest tightened with worry, but running away wasn't a viable plan, and I needed to take the Scarab down here and now. Then I could deal with whatever—or whoever—else might be targeting me.

But how could I defeat an armored machine? My stormsword was still in the locker room, and the chunk of rock I'd used to disable the camera had shattered to shards when it hit the ground.

My gaze flicked from one thing to another, even as my mind churned, searching for something, anything, I could use as a weapon. The topiary trees and hedges were no help. Neither were the marble statues . . .

My seer magic surged, and a flare of silver caught my eye. I spun in that direction, and my gaze landed on the mermaid statue in the center of the biodome. Why would my magic point out the statue? I could sense Kyrion's telekinesis much more easily than before, but the psionic dampeners were still active, and the white fog hadn't completely dissipated from my mind. I might have been able to toss the rock to take down the camera, but I couldn't access enough of Kyrion's power to throw the large, heavy mermaid statue at the Scarab.

Wait. Maybe I didn't have to use the whole statue. My eyes narrowed, and I focused on the trident the mermaid was clutching. Unlike the rest of the smooth white marble statue, the trident was made of metal and featured three long, pointed ends that reminded me of the tines on a fork.

My heart rose with hope, but it quickly sank right back down again. The mermaid was gripping the trident, and there was no way I could pry her stone fingers off the hilt with my own strength. I might have been able to do it with Kyrion's telekinesis, but it would have taken an enormous amount of magic, and I didn't want to risk draining off too much of his power, especially since I didn't know what enemies he might be battling.

More branches cracked, and the Scarab finally extricated itself from the topiary tree. The machine crashed around, splintering the heavy branches underfoot. My eyes narrowed again, and my mind whirred, calculating distances and angles. I couldn't wrest the trident out of the mermaid's stone grip, but maybe the Scarab could.

"Hey, you!" I yelled. "Circuits for brains! Come and get me!"

I waved my hand and moved to the right, putting myself between the Scarab and the mermaid statue. The Scarab spun around, and its green eyes brightened, as though whoever was controlling the machine was determined to finally latch onto me.

"Hey!" I yelled again. "You want me? Then come and get me!"

The Scarab's eyes brightened even more, and the machine rushed forward. I braced myself and waited for the Scarab to come closer.

At the last instant, right before the machine would have slammed into me, I lunged to the side. The Scarab crashed directly into the mermaid, and the statue shattered on impact. Chunks of white marble sailed through the air like misshapen snowballs, as did the trident, which chimed against the ground like a tuning fork.

While the Scarab careened to a halt, I darted forward and snatched up the trident. It was made of solid silver and even heavier and sturdier than I'd expected. Even better, each of the three large prongs ended in a razor-sharp point.

Clank. Clank-clank. Clank.

The Scarab whirled around and charged in my direction.

My eyes narrowed, and I once again calculated distances and angles. The Scarab rushed forward and stretched its arm out toward me . . .

I spun to the side and stabbed out with the trident. My aim was true, and I drove the three prongs deep into the machine's left knee before ripping them right back out. The Scarab tripped and went down in a heap, tumbling end over end, cracking flagstones and sending up sprays of stone shrapnel in its wake.

The second the machine slid to a halt, I darted forward and raised the trident again. First, I stabbed the prongs into the machine's right knee, tearing through its armor, along with the wires underneath. The Scarab tried to stand, but its crippled knees wouldn't support the rest of its heavy weight, and it toppled down and landed on its back.

The Scarab swiped a hand at me, but I ignored the awkward lurch and rammed the trident into the machine's right elbow, then its left elbow. With four quick strikes, I'd essentially turned the deadly machine into a black bug lying on its shell, fruitlessly kicking its ruined arms and legs in the air.

Once I was certain the Scarab couldn't get back up, I leaned over the machine, raised the trident high, and stabbed it into the center of the Scarab's breastplate. The prongs didn't penetrate as deeply as I'd hoped, so I wrenched the trident back and forth in short, violent motions. Several satisfying *snaps*, *cracks*, and *pop-pop-pops* rang out as the prongs tore through the machine's innards.

After several vicious twists, I yanked the trident free. The Scarab's arms and legs fell limply to its sides, and not so much as a single mechanical finger twitched. I had disabled the awful machine.

I stepped forward and bent down so that I was staring into the Scarab's eyes, which were still glowing a bright, vivid green. Just like with the overhead camera, I got the sense of someone looking at me through the lenses. My skin crawled with a mixture of anger and revulsion.

"I don't know who you are or what you want, but we're playing *my* game now," I snarled. "And you're going to lose a lot more than just this blasted machine."

The Scarab's eyes widened, almost as if whoever was on the other side of the lenses was gaping in shock. I raised the trident high and buried the prongs in the Scarab's right eye.

Pewp!

A strange electronic wail erupted from the machine, almost as if it was begging for mercy, and its entire body shuddered, as though I had just struck the most vital part of it. The green lights flickered, dimmed, and died in its eyes, and the Scarab sagged against the ground. I yanked the trident free, raised a shaking hand, and wiped the sweat off my forehead.

A flare of light caught my eye. I tensed and straightened up. For a moment, I thought my magic was pointing out another object or enemy, but this time, the light was coming from the holocuff clamped around my wrist. The device was showing my rapid heart rate, and I was willing to bet it was still transmitting my hologram to the control room, along with my location in the maze.

I crouched down, set the trident aside, and grabbed a chunk of the mermaid statue. Then I smashed the jagged stone onto the holoscreen embedded in the silver cuff.

Crack!

The screen shattered, but I kept going, hammering at the surrounding metal again and again.

Crack!

I finally hit the locking mechanism, and the cuff popped open and dropped from my wrist. Disgust curled through me, and I stood up and kicked it away.

"Try tracking me now," I snarled.

I plucked the trident off the ground and once again considered my options. I could move deeper into the maze and try to find Kyrion, or I could go back the way I'd come and try to figure out what was going on in the facility.

Kyrion? Kyrion!

I called out, but he didn't answer me, and I didn't get the sense I was any closer to him. Frustration and worry pounded through my body in equal measure, but I forced myself to think coldly and logically.

As much as I wanted to find Kyrion, I was closer to the maze exit than I was to him. Plus, I didn't know how many more Scarabs or other enemies might be between us. The smartest course of action was to backtrack and get out of the maze.

I hesitated, torn about leaving Kyrion behind, but the rogue Arrow could take care of himself. Right now, I needed to figure out exactly who and what we were up against. I also needed to learn what had happened to Siya and Asterin. My friends would *never* unleash a real Black Scarab on me, not even in a training exercise. Every instinct I had was screaming that someone else was controlling the maze, which meant Siya and Asterin were in just as much danger as Kyrion and I were in.

I stared at the path that led out of the far side of the biodome and deeper into the maze. *I'm coming back for you, Kyr, just as soon as I can.*

There was no response, and I had no idea if he'd heard my whispered words or teasing nickname. But just making the promise sent fresh purpose, strength, and determination flowing through me. It was time to get out of this blasted maze and find out who was really pulling the strings around here.

My hand clenched around the hilt of the silver trident, and I twirled the weapon around into an attack position. Then I stepped over the lifeless shell of the Black Scarab, left the garden biodome behind, and went back the way I'd come.

ELEVEN

VESPER

I quickly backtracked through the maze.

One of the good things about being a seer was that I never forgot anything I saw, did, or experienced, so it was easy for me to remember the twists and turns. I retraced my steps to the entrance only to find the wall was still in place, trapping me inside. Annoyance shot through me. Of course it was.

Nothing in the galaxy could ever be that blasted *easy*.

I ran my fingers over the wall, but the metal was thick and solid, and there was no way I could move the heavy slab, not even with Kyrion's telekinesis. Next, I went over and gave several experimental yanks on the honeysuckle vines clinging to a nearby wall. The thick vines might form a solid mass, but they tore down easily, and they simply weren't strong enough to support my weight and let me climb up and over the slick wall.

I let out a frustrated snarl and paced back and forth. One blasted wall stood between me and . . . well, *freedom* wasn't the right word, but I'd rather be outside the maze than inside it.

Think, Vesper, think!

I kept pacing, studying the wall the same way I would a faulty brewmaker or a misfiring blaster in the R&D lab, but there wasn't much to see. Just a big ol' slab of metal perched on tracks that let it slide back and forth.

My eyes narrowed, and I studied the tracks a little more closely. The maze might be controlled from exterior panels, but in the R&D lab, buttons failed, levers snapped, and circuits fried all the time. The House Battis technicians would have had to install a manual release *inside* the maze to move the wall in case of an emergency or catastrophic control or power failure.

I quit looking at the exit, spun around, and stabbed my stolen trident into the honeysuckle vines on the left side of the path. The sharp tips sheared through the vines and revealed the smooth metal wall underneath. No release here.

Frustration filled me, but I whirled around and moved over to the right side of the path. I repeated the process and stabbed the trident into the honeysuckle vines.

Tink.

The prongs bounced off something jutting out from the wall. Excitement coursed through me, and I used the trident like a pitchfork to tear down thick wads of vines. A few seconds later, I uncovered a metal box painted the same green as the honeysuckle vines. Jackpot.

The box had a hole for a key I didn't have, so I jammed the trident prongs into the seam between the door and the rest of the box. Then I leaned my body weight on the trident, using it like a lever.

Screech!

The lock broke, and the door popped open, revealing a small metal wheel nestled inside the box. I set the trident down, grabbed the wheel with both hands, and turned it. The wheel resisted, like it had never been used, so I dug my boots into the ground and put more of my strength into the motion.

I also reached for the bond again, grabbed the tiny trickles of Kyrion's telekinesis, and added his power to my own.

The wheel slowly turned one inch, then two, then three . . .

Screech!

The wheel finally turned all the way, and the metal wall slid back. I redoubled my efforts and kept twisting the wheel until I had created a gap large enough to slip through. I grinned and pumped my fist in the air in triumph.

Vesper 1, Maze 0.

I grabbed the trident, then tiptoed forward and peered through the opening. No Black Scarabs were waiting outside, and no one was at the control panel Siya had used earlier.

I drew in a breath, then stepped out of the maze. A sharp, tingling sensation swept over my skin, like I had just sloughed off some unwanted dirt, and the dull background roar finally faded from my ears. I exhaled with relief. I was clear of the psionic dampeners, so my senses were back to normal, although that mental white fog was still wisping between me and Kyrion, who was still deep in the maze.

I held my position, looking and listening in case this was another trap, but I didn't see anything out of the ordinary, and the only sounds were the faint hisses of the fog machines in the distance. My gaze lifted to the upper level, but no one was standing along the railing.

Siya? Asterin? I called out telepathically, but neither one of them responded, and no strong emotions rippled through the air.

Worry twisted my stomach, but I clutched the trident a little tighter and left the maze behind. First I was going to find my friends, and then I was going to deal with whoever had been stupid enough to target us.

Keeping an eye out for more Black Scarabs, I went over to

the control panel. The holoscreens were dark, and none of the buttons lit up or did anything, no matter how many times I punched them. None of the knobs and switches responded either. The panel was dead, which meant someone was manipulating the maze from the main panel in the control room.

And they were looking for me.

Several cameras zoomed down from the ceiling and tilted their lenses toward the maze. Wide red beams of light shot out from the bottoms of the cameras as they slowly moved back and forth, scanning each part of the maze. The lights were probably some kind of thermal imaging designed to pick up my heat signature in case I was hiding in the honeysuckle vines or one of the biodomes. None of the cameras was near the exit, but it was only a matter of time before my mysterious enemy realized the mouse had escaped their trap.

Since the control panel was dead, I went over to the door that led to the stairs. Locked. A keypad was embedded in the wall, but I had no idea what the code was—

Pew! Pew! Pew!

The sharp sounds of blaster fire zipped through the air. My heart leaped into my throat, and I spun around, expecting bright, deadly streaks of electricity to come zinging toward me and slam into my chest.

But the area was still deserted, and no one sprinted out of the maze brandishing a weapon.

Pew! Pew! Pew!

More blaster fire rang out. My heart climbed a little higher up my throat, but the sharp sounds quickly vanished. I drew in a deep breath, but no ozone aroma flooded my nose. The blaster fire must be on the far side of the maze—where Kyrion was.

Kyr? Are you okay? Kyr!

I called out with as much force and magic as I could. He didn't answer, but the sticky cobweb of him practically steamed with anger.

My heart twisted with worry. I stepped toward the maze, but I forced myself to stop. As much as I wanted to charge back inside and find Kyrion, the best thing I could do for both of us was to figure out exactly what was going on, so I reluctantly turned back toward the keypad.

First step: Get through this door. I jammed the trident prongs in between the concrete wall and the plastic casing that covered the keypad. After a few forceful wiggles, the casing popped off the wall and clattered to the ground. I set the trident aside and stared at the nest of colored wires curled around the keypad.

A sense of calm settled over me, like I was back in the R&D lab tinkering with a new blaster design. I embraced the feeling and did the same thing I would have done in the lab—I traced my fingers along the wires, seeing where they plugged into the keypad, along with the surrounding circuitry.

Lucky for me, the wires were covered with a cheap plastic coating that I was able to peel away with my fingernails. I quickly exposed several wires, then touched them together. Sparks zinged through the air, along with the crackle of electricity, but I kept testing one combination of wires after another after another . . .

Beep!

The light on the keypad turned green, and the door buzzed open. I pumped my fist in the air in triumph again.

Vesper 2, Maze 0.

Pew! Pew! Pew!

Another round of blaster fire erupted in the maze, and an instant later, a sharp spike of pain stabbed into my right forearm. The force of the phantom blow knocked me back against the wall hard enough to rattle my teeth and make me bite my tongue.

Blast it. That had *hurt*.

I yanked up my jacket and shirtsleeves, knowing and dreading what I would find. Sure enough, an angry red burn had appeared on my right forearm. My heart pounded in my chest, matching the rapid, painful throb of the wound.

Kyrion had been shot.

When our truebond had first formed, we often mirrored each other's injuries. If I cut my hand on a dagger, a similar mark would appear on the same spot on Kyrion's hand, although his wound usually wouldn't be as deep or painful as the actual cut on my hand. After we had finally accepted our truebond in the Crownpoint throne room several weeks ago, I thought we would stop mirroring each other's injuries, but I was wrong.

Sometimes if I clipped my shoulder on a doorway or bruised my knee on a table, the same injury would appear on Kyrion's body, and vice versa if he rammed his elbow into a shelf or landed awkwardly on his hip during sparring. But other times when Kyrion and I injured ourselves, the physical marks would only appear on the injured person's body, and the other person didn't experience any psionic echoes of pain.

I'd started keeping track of which injuries appeared, along with their severity, but so far, there was no rhyme, reason, or discernible pattern to how, why, or when our wounds mirrored each other and when they didn't. The lack of clear action and reaction was another frustrating facet of the ever-evolving puzzle of having a truebond. Just when I thought I had finally figured something out, something else arose that completely upended my perception of my magic, Kyrion's power, and everything else that came with our connection.

But the severity of this injury told me exactly how much Kyrion was hurting—and how dangerous his enemy was. This wasn't the mild redness from a blaster set to stun. No, that bolt had been designed to incapacitate Kyrion, at best, and kill him, at worst. Dread pounded through my body.

I'm coming, Kyr! Hang on!

I sent the thought, although yet again, I had no idea if he heard it. The sticky cobweb of Kyrion bristled with even more anger, although that emotion was quickly iced over by a cold, ruthless determination I recognized all too well.

Kyrion Caldaren might be injured, but he was far from defeated, and the rogue Arrow was going to make his enemy pay. An answering determination swept through me, and a sharp grin split my lips.

Me too, Kyr. Me too.

I grabbed my trident and held it out in front of me. Then I stepped through the open door to continue my search for the spider controlling this dangerous web.

TWELVE

KYRION

I charged forward, my boots thumping against the flagstones. Roderick Battis knew the maze like the back of his hand, and my only course of action was to retreat along the paths I had already explored, reach the outer wall, and escape. Once I was free of the psionic dampeners, I should be able to sense exactly where Vesper was and clearly communicate with her.

I sprinted along one path after another, but it didn't take me long to realize this was one race I was going to lose. Roderick's armored boots must have had a propulsion system to increase his speed, because his footsteps were quickly growing louder and closer. The Hammer was swiftly running me down, and I wasn't going to be able to escape the maze before he caught me. Change of plan. I was going to have to make a stand and fight Roderick on his own turf.

Up ahead, another junction appeared. I didn't have time to stop, look around, and study my options, so I took the right path. I rounded a long, large curve, entered a biodome, and skidded to a halt.

My gaze snapped back and forth. Honeysuckle vines, blue-moon peonies, and other flowers, marble statues, stone fountains, but no energy shield overhead. This was the same garden biodome where Roderick had confronted me a few minutes ago. Fuck. I thought I'd been heading toward the outer edge of the maze, but instead, I'd just run around in a giant circle.

A sharp whistle shrieked out, making me flinch in surprise. The sound intensified with each passing second, like a high-speed train was bearing down on me. On instinct, I lunged to my right.

Crack!

Roderick's war hammer slammed into one of the House Battis castle statues. The black marble exploded at the hard, jarring impact, and red sparks shot up into the air like fireworks. I lifted my hand and threw up a psionic shield, using my telekinesis to send the sharp shards of stone spinning away from me.

The hammer plowed through the air until it hit one of the honeysuckle-covered walls. The weapon bounced off the metal underneath the greenery and dropped to the ground. Roderick sprinted into the biodome, stopped, and snapped his hand forward. A wave of telekinesis rolled off him, and the hammer lifted off the ground.

I whirled toward Roderick and reached out with my own telekinesis. If I could get my hands on the hammer, then I could crack through the other warrior's armor and break every rib in his chest.

Sparks of red and blue fire crackled, hissed, and shot off the lunarium weapon, and the hammer zigzagged wildly back and forth through the air as Roderick and I played tug-of-war with our telekinesis. I snarled and lashed out with even more power. The lunarium turned more blue than red, and the hammer lurched in my direction.

Roderick growled and made a scooping motion with his

left hand. A chunk of stone from the smashed statue lifted off the ground and hurtled toward my face. I jerked to the side. The stone sailed through the air where my head had been, but the motion broke my concentration, and the hammer streaked through the air and settled into Roderick's hand.

"You're already so desperate." The other warrior clucked his tongue in mock sympathy. "I expected more from the infamous Kyrion Caldaren."

Roderick twirled the hammer around in his hand, then dug his boots into the ground and launched himself at me.

Suddenly, Vesper's seer power surged, even though I wasn't trying to use her ability. Time slowed down, as though I was watching battle footage one frame at a time on a holoscreen, and one thing after another caught my eye. The glossy gleam of Roderick's armor. His knuckles bulging as he clutched the golden hilt of his war hammer. The lunarium weapon glowing a vivid, angry red in a reflection of his psion power . . .

Time snapped back to its normal flow, and Vesper's power sluiced off me like water. At the last moment, right before Roderick would have smashed his hammer into my chest, I snapped up my hands, grabbed hold of the statue rubble, and flung it at him.

The heavy stones punched into Roderick's chest, knocking him off course. The other warrior hit a wall and bounced off. He landed hard on his knees, although his Scarab armor absorbed the bruising impact.

Roderick's head snapped up, and he quickly climbed to his feet. His dark brown eyes gleamed almost as brightly as his lunarium hammer, and another wide grin split his face like he was wearing a grotesque mask that showed every single one of his perfect white teeth.

He was *enjoying* this. Everything I did to fight back and keep myself alive fed into his sick fantasy that he was an alpha warrior and the ultimate hunter. Sadistic bastard.

My inner monster roared with rage. I snarled, lifted my hand, and grabbed more of the statue rubble with my telekinesis. I threw chunk after chunk of stone at Roderick, but he used his hammer to bat the debris away.

I reached for even more of my telekinesis, throwing the stones faster and faster. Roderick snarled and upped his own tempo in response, but his hammer was still a large, heavy weapon and much harder—and slower—to wield than the rubble.

A chunk of stone flew past Roderick's defenses and clipped his left shoulder. Another chunk battered his right thigh, then two more chunks slammed into the center of his chest and knocked him back. Once again, Roderick's armor absorbed the brunt of the blows, but he had to lower his hammer to maintain his balance.

I snarled again and stalked forward, pressing my advantage. All I had to do was bean the other warrior in the head and daze him. Then I could rip the war hammer out of his hand and beat him to death with his own weapon.

Roderick regained his balance and glowered at me, as though I'd upset his script for how this was supposed to play out. He lifted his left forearm to his lips. "Activate the blasters in section forty-seven!" he yelled at the holoscreen embedded in the armor.

From the corner of my eye, I saw a glint of metal jutting out of a wall. I whirled in that direction.

Pew! Pew! Pew!

Blaster fire zinged out from the hidden nozzle. I spun to my right, avoiding the sizzling orange bolts, which slammed into a cluster of blue-moon peonies and blew them to pieces.

More bolts zinged through the air. I tried to spin out of the way again, but my boots slipped on some broken stones, and I staggered directly into the line of fire. I gritted my teeth and snapped my hands up, using my telekinesis to deflect the dangerous streaks of electricity.

Pew! Pew! Pew!

One of the bolts slipped past my defenses and slammed into my right forearm. Hot, electric agony exploded in my arm, sizzling down into my fingers and up into my shoulder. The acrid stench of my own burning skin flooded my nose, my heart pounded, and my stomach roiled with nausea.

I immediately threw up a psionic shield, walling off the hot, pulsing agony in a small, distant corner of my mind, but a different kind of pain rose to take its place. The velvety ribbon of Vesper in my mind stiffened in shock, as though she too had felt the sharp sting and intense burn. I grimaced. As much as I enjoyed being connected to Vesper, I hated that our truebond exposed her to so much of my physical pain.

But Vesper's shock made me even more determined to kill Roderick. This sadistic bastard was not laying a single finger on her. My inner monster snarled with rage, and an answering growl rumbled out of my throat.

To my surprise, Roderick threw his head back and laughed. "What a fun game," he crooned. "Let's see just how much damage you can take, Kyrion."

I clenched my hands into fists and lunged at the mocking lord, but he darted away from me.

"Activate secondary wave!" he commanded, although I couldn't tell if he was talking to the holoscreen on his forearm, or Jeffrey, or both.

Another glint of metal appeared on a different wall, and a second nozzle jutted out of the greenery.

Pew! Pew! Pew!

More blaster bolts zinged through the air. I ducked behind a bubbling fountain and let it take the brunt of the blasts.

Pew! Pew! Pew!

Water sprayed everywhere, and chips of stone cracked off the fountain, zipped through the air, and stung my head, face, neck, and hands like angry wasps. Between the two blaster nozzles, I was in danger of being pinned down, something I couldn't afford with Roderick still clutching his hammer and creeping closer.

"What's the matter, Kyrion? Did you really think I was going to play fair?" Roderick called out in a mocking voice. "A hunt would only be fair if the hunter gave the animal a weapon, and we both know that's *never* going to happen."

Anger sizzled in my chest, but it was quickly extinguished by cold, ruthless determination. Roderick didn't need to give me a weapon. I was an Arrow, an assassin, and one of the best warriors in the galaxy. I had spent years surviving one battle after another, whether it was a physical fight against Techwave soldiers or a psychological duel against Callus Holloway, who never failed to twist a verbal knife in my gut.

I didn't need a weapon—I *was* the weapon.

Pew! Pew! Pew!

Blaster bolts kept streaking through the air, obliterating more and more of the fountain. I couldn't stay here. If the bolts didn't kill me, then Roderick would with his hammer. I needed to get out of this biodome and find Vesper.

Pew! Pew! Pew!

Another round of bolts slammed into the fountain. The instant they stopped, I surged to my feet, snapped my hands up, and grabbed as many chunks of rubble as I could with my telekinesis. Then I flung my hands and my power out and sent all those pieces hurtling toward the blasters.

Crack! Crack!

Crack! Crack!

The chunks of stone slammed into the blaster traps. One nozzle exploded at the impact. A ball of fire streaked upward, and the surrounding honeysuckle vines smoldered, adding an oddly sweet perfume to the ozone stench in the air.

A chunk of stone clipped the edge of the second nozzle, making it spin in the opposite direction.

Pew! Pew! Pew!

This time, Roderick was the one who had to duck blaster bolts. He cursed and threw himself down onto the ground behind a castle statue, despite the armor he was wearing.

The bolts kept zinging in Roderick's direction, pinning him in place. I whirled around and sprinted for the nearest path, heading away from my enemy and into a different, unknown section of the maze.

THIRTEEN

VESPER

Still clutching the trident, I quickly climbed the spiral stairs. Any moment, I expected an enemy to pop into view, but no one appeared, and the only sounds were my raspy breaths and soft footsteps.

I reached the door at the top of the stairs and tugged on the handle. To my surprise, it was unlocked. I waited a few seconds, but when no alarms blared, I opened the door a little wider and peered around the side. The corridor beyond was empty. No one realized I'd gotten out of the maze and up to the control level. Good.

I stepped through to the other side, put my back up against the wall, and sidled down the corridor. I glanced up at the ceiling, but none of the security cameras tracked my movements. Judging from the lack of red lights burning on the devices, the cameras had been turned off. Of course they were off. Whoever was behind this wouldn't want a recording of themselves going through the facility, just of Kyrion and me being attacked in the maze. Anger sparked in my chest, spurring me onward.

I moved from one corridor to the next, hugging the walls and keeping my steps as silent as possible. Given the late hour, most of the lights had been dimmed, probably thanks to an automated system designed to save electricity, and I stayed in the shadows.

Finally, I came to the junction where the corridor flowed into the main, wide space that led to the locker room, the armory, the infirmary, and, most important of all, the control room. Up ahead, around the corner, a series of soft *tap-tap-taps* rang out. Someone was typing on a holoscreen.

My fingers tightened around the trident. I tiptoed up to the edge of the junction, then crouched down and peered around the corner.

Unlike on the rest of this level, which was cloaked in shadows, lights blazed in the control room at the far end of the corridor. Jeffrey, the House Battis technician, was still ensconced in front of the main panel, swiping through holograms and looking at one monitor and camera feed after another.

"Where is she?" he muttered. "Where the fuck did she go?"

Jeffrey kept looking at the feeds, which showed different sections of the maze. Off to his left, two holograms flickered in the air. One was a tall, hulking figure in red armor I didn't recognize, but the other was clearly Kyrion, who was running through the maze.

My heart squeezed tight, but I pushed my worry aside. I couldn't help Kyrion right now, but I could help Siya and Asterin.

The two women were standing behind Jeffrey. Cuts and bruises crisscrossed Siya's face and her knuckles, while Asterin's lower lip was split and her long black hair was half in and half out of its ponytail, like someone had given it a vicious yank.

Siya was positioned on one side of a table, while Asterin was on the opposite side. Wide metal cuffs circled their wrists, and a thick chain shackled their hands together in front of them and then down to the table. Red lights also burned on the cuffs, indicating that they were equipped with psionic power dampeners.

Four House Battis Hammers, two men and two women, were guarding Siya and Asterin. All the warriors were carrying lunarium war hammers. My silver trident might have let me kill the Black Scarab in the maze, but it was no match against the other warriors' weapons. I needed my stormsword, but it was still in the locker room, and there was no way I could creep down the corridor and slip into that area without the Hammers seeing me.

"You'll never get away with this," Siya hissed.

Jeffrey rolled his eyes. "Please. Roderick has been getting away with this for *years*. Your friends aren't the first truebonded couple he's hunted through the maze."

Roderick? My gaze flicked back to the hologram of the red-armored figure, and I finally recognized the Erzton lord.

The more exotic and dangerous the creature, the better . . . Roderick's hunts are cruel and barbaric, just like he is . . . Siya's voice whispered through my mind.

She had been more right about him than she knew. Given Jeffrey's snide words, it sounded like Roderick had grown tired of hunting animals long ago, and tonight he'd decided to make Kyrion and me his latest victims. No doubt he thought our truebond made us the rarest of creatures. White-hot rage streaked through my chest like a shooting star. Well, we were going to be the last people he ever terrorized. If Kyrion didn't kill Roderick, then I would.

A thought bubbled up in my mind, cooling my rage. Roderick might be stalking Kyrion through the maze, but the Black Scarab had clearly been trying to capture me instead of killing me. Why would Roderick want me alive?

"How are you going to explain what happened to us?"

Asterin asked, her voice low, tight, and furious. "People from House Collier don't just *disappear*. And Siya is the heir. She would *never* abandon her House."

Jeffrey chuckled. "People from the major Houses disappear every day, including heirs. But by the time other folks realize something is wrong, it's too late." He glanced over his shoulder and sneered at my friends. "Just like it's too late for the two of you."

Asterin fell silent, as did Siya, although they both kept glaring at the technician.

My gaze skipped from one thing to another. Asterin and Siya cuffed to the table. The four Hammers guarding them. Jeffrey flipping switches at the control panel like a musician playing a familiar instrument.

Storming into the control room was not an option. I couldn't help my friends, much less Kyrion, if I was captured—or dead.

"I've already arranged a tragic transport accident that will burn your bodies to a crisp," Jeffrey continued. "One of the Hammers is planting the explosives on your ship right now. The only question is whether Roderick will kill you before the Hammers put you on board or have them strap you in the transport while you're still alive."

A cruel grin curved his lips, and his brown eyes gleamed with malice. "Me? I'm voting for alive just so I can hear you scream."

Asterin's face paled, and Siya muttered a curse.

My ears perked up. Explosives? I could use some explosives right now.

Jeffrey smirked at Asterin and Siya a moment longer, then turned back to the control panel and starting swiping through holograms again. "I still can't believe that truebond bitch took down my Scarab. It was the only one I had, and I just started testing it last week. I was still tweaking the controls."

His voice took on a high, whiny note like he was a child

whose favorite action figure had been broken. Well, I was just getting started, and I was going to destroy a lot more than just his precious Scarab. But first, I had to let my friends know I was here.

I reached for the bond. *Asterin? Asterin, can you hear me?*

My friend frowned and glanced over at Siya, like the other warrior was the one speaking. I ground my teeth. Most of the time, I could easily communicate with Kyrion, given our bond, but I was still having trouble using his telepathy to contact other people. Plus, he was still in the maze, surrounded by psionic dampeners, which made it even more difficult than usual.

I grabbed as many trickles of Kyrion's magic as I could through the mental white fog still wisping between us and focused on Asterin's face and the sound of her name in my mind.

Asterin? Asterin!

My friend grimaced like I'd just shouted in her ear. She glanced at the Hammers guarding her and Siya, then over at Jeffrey. Finally, she looked past the technician. She scanned the corridor, and her eyes widened as she caught sight of me crouching in the shadows.

Asterin waggled her fingers at Siya, then tilted her head the slightest bit in my direction. Siya frowned, but she too scanned the corridor and caught sight of me in the shadows.

Siya's hazel eyes narrowed, and she jerked her head in a sharp motion. She clearly wanted me to sneak out of the facility and go get help. That probably was the smartest, safest thing to do, but I wasn't leaving. Not while my friends were in danger and especially not while Kyrion was trapped in the maze with Roderick hunting him like he was a Tropics tiger.

Jeffrey glanced over his shoulder at the two women. "What are you doing?"

"Nothing," Asterin muttered. "Thanks to these blasted cuffs."

She lifted her hands and yanked on the attached chain, but the metal links remained securely fastened to the table.

Jeffrey studied Asterin, then Siya, who gave him a flat look in return. Neither of my friends glanced in my direction, but the four Hammers drifted forward and hefted their weapons. I held my breath and carefully lifted my trident into an attack position, ready to charge forward to help my friends if the Hammers attacked.

After a few more seconds of silent scrutiny, Jeffrey turned back to the control panel and started swiping through the camera feeds again. The Hammers also lowered their weapons.

I exhaled, but my relief was short-lived. It wouldn't be long before the cameras finished sweeping over the maze and Jeffrey realized that I was loose in the facility. I needed to put my plan into action before that happened.

I'll be back soon. I sent the thought to Asterin.

She still didn't look at me, but her chin dipped slightly, indicating she had heard me.

Worry churned through my stomach about leaving Asterin and Siya behind, but I needed more weapons if I had any hope of rescuing them, so I drew back into the shadows, got to my feet, and left the area.

I hurried down the corridor to the closest junction. A couple of signs on the wall pointed the way to the transport garage, so I headed in that direction. Luck was on my side, and the double doors were standing wide open.

The garage was a large, cavernous space made of dull gray concrete. Several transports were spaced throughout the area, while counters filled with tools, wheels, solar batteries, and more hugged the walls. Skid marks blackened the floor, and the scents of greasy oil and smoky exhaust clouded the air. At the far end, the two enormous metal doors that served as the entrance and exit for the ships were closed.

I scuttled forward and ducked behind a massive transport bearing a House Battis sigil that had to belong to Roderick. Up ahead, someone was whistling a loud, cheerful tune. Using Roderick's spaceship for cover, I followed the noise deeper into the garage. I came to the end of the ship, crouched down, and peered around the side.

The House Collier transport we had ridden in to the training facility was right where Siya had parked it. A man dressed in a red House Battis uniform was standing at a nearby table, fiddling with a black box that had three green lights, a small silver antenna, and a red switch. That must be the detonator for the explosives, which were most likely housed in another, much larger black box that was perched on the table.

I needed to get both the detonator and the box of explosives for my plan to work, so I got to my feet and moved forward.

I slid past one transport after another, circling around the perimeter of the garage until I was almost directly behind the Hammer. I drew in a deep breath, then let it out, raised my trident, and charged forward.

The Hammer whirled around at the sound of my boots slapping against the floor. His eyes widened in surprise, and the small detonator slipped through his fingers and clattered to the table. He cursed, then lunged forward and fumbled for a blaster lying on the far end of the table.

I quickened my pace, crossed the distance between us, and rammed the trident into his chest. The man screamed, and his sharp shriek of pain boomed out as loud as, well, a bomb in the enclosed space.

I grimaced, yanked the trident out, and pulled it back for another strike, but the Hammer staggered to the side, hit the wall, and bounced off it. His feet flew out from under him, his legs buckled, and his head cracked against the edge of the table. His screams abruptly cut off, and he dropped to the floor like a stone tossed into a pond.

Blood gushed out of the Hammer's chest and the deep gash on his head. His arms and legs twitched for a few seconds, then stilled. His head lolled to the side, his gaze already fixed.

I waited a few seconds, making sure he was dead, then glanced back over my shoulder. No shouts or footsteps sounded, and no one rushed into the garage. No one had seen or heard me kill the other warrior. Good.

I set my trident aside, crouched down, and rifled through the Hammer's pockets. He was carrying a tablet, and I had to resist the urge to kiss the electronic device. I picked up the dead man's limp hand and pressed his thumb against the screen. The tablet unlocked, and I quickly keyed in an identification number.

Most folks didn't bother memorizing other people's ID numbers anymore, but I always did. Thanks to my many years as a lab rat, I knew just how easily technology could break, fail, and malfunction, and it was always better to know the information yourself than to rely on a tablet to retrieve it. Plus, my seer magic made it easy to memorize whatever I wanted.

I typed a message to Rigel, who was Siya's second-in-command of the House Collier Hammers. I told Rigel where we were, what was happening, and what I planned to do about it all. Then I set the tablet to silent and slid it into my pocket. Rigel would get here as fast as possible, but the Collier estate was on a neighboring mountain, and Kyrion, Asterin, and Siya didn't have time for me to wait for backup.

I rifled through the rest of the dead man's pockets, but he didn't have anything else useful. Next, I got to my feet and studied the two black boxes on the table. Just as I'd suspected, the large box contained a signal receiver and some blasting caps buried in the middle of several explosive bricks, while the small box was the signal transmitter and detonator. In the Quill Corp R&D lab, we often blew up brewmakers and other appliances to test how sturdy and resilient they were, so I was familiar with the items.

Judging from the green lights on both devices, the Hammer had already synced them together, so all I had to do was flip the red switch on the detonator, and *boom*!

I grinned. I finally had some serious firepower, and I knew just how to use it.

FOURTEEN

KYRION

I sprinted down one path after another, plunging deeper and deeper into the maze.

I didn't have time to look for traps, but no more blaster nozzles appeared, and nothing else slowed my progress. Even if I had blundered into an obstacle and been injured, I would have kept going. Right now, all I cared about was finding Vesper and making sure she was safe from the Black Scarab and whatever other horrors Roderick and Jeffrey might have unleashed.

Vesper? Vesper!

Her voice didn't sound in my mind, and the velvety ribbon of her felt even smaller and thinner, as though only the longest, tiniest strand connected us. Why would she suddenly feel so much farther away?

Unless . . . Vesper had gotten out of the maze.

As soon as the thought entered my mind, I knew it was true—I could *feel* it was true.

My inner monster hissed with relief, and the dark cloud of

dread hanging over my head evaporated. Vesper had escaped. Even more telling, the velvety ribbon of her vibrated with determination. Wherever she was and whatever she was doing, she had a plan of attack.

A wide grin stretched across my face. Vesper Quill with a plan was one of the most dangerous things in the whole bloody galaxy, and I almost felt sorry for whoever had been stupid enough to get in her way. Almost.

If Vesper didn't kill our enemies, then I would, including Roderick, Jeffrey, and everyone else associated with this house of horrors.

I kept sprinting through the maze, but now, instead of frantically looking for Vesper and trying to escape, I started searching for a place to make a stand against my enemy. Roderick and I were in the middle of an obstacle course, and it was time to put some obstacles in *his* path.

I moved from one section of the maze to another, only pausing long enough at the junctions to peer down the various paths. By this point, I had lost all sense of direction, and I had no idea where I was in the maze. I needed to find a biodome with statues, trees, fountains, or other big, blunt, heavy objects I could use as weapons.

Whenever I came to a junction, I also paused long enough to listen, but I didn't hear Roderick's footsteps anymore. He was probably relishing the chance to slowly, quietly stalk me through the maze like I was one of those Frozon wolves he loved to hunt.

But I wasn't a wolf, I was a monster, and I wasn't even close to being defeated.

After reaching a dead end and having to backtrack, I veered onto a different path and finally stepped into another biodome. This biodome was much, much larger than the other areas, and I could tell it was the center of the maze. And just like the other biodomes, it too had a themed environment with a very distinctive feature: lava.

Long, rectangular, knee-high permaglass pools filled with lava lined the wide flagstone paths that crisscrossed the ground. Waist-high bronze cauldrons also filled with lava were scattered here and there, while several more pools and cauldrons ringed a circular space in the middle of the biodome that reminded me of a gladiator arena. The pools and cauldrons must have been treated to withstand and contain the extreme element, although the glass and bronze containers still glowed with heat.

Shock sliced through my gut. This biodome was modeled after a Magma planet. A red-hot heart at the heart of the maze. Cute, ironic, and extremely dangerous.

The lava just reinforced how arrogant Roderick was. Only someone with an exceptionally large ego would be foolish enough to try to contain and control such a deadly element, even in a training facility.

A bubble rose in the lava in a glass pool and abruptly popped, blasting steam into the air. More bubbles rose and popped in the other pools and cauldrons, releasing even more suffocating steam. No honeysuckle vines adorned the walls, and many of the flagstones had cracked from the intense heat. Even the energy shield overhead continually bucked and heaved, like it was trying to stuff the steam back down into the lava. I'd only been here for a few seconds, and my skin felt drenched with sweat and bone-dry at the same time.

Vesper would have appreciated the ingenuity of pumping lava into the middle of the maze without destroying the surrounding paths, flowers, and biodomes, but my lips curled back in disgust, and a snarl rumbled out of my throat.

As an Arrow, not much scared me, but I would never forget how the ground had cracked open like an eggshell and released geysers of lava during the Techwave battle on Magma 7 several months ago. A shudder rippled through my body. I would have died in that field of lava if Vesper hadn't used her seer magic to steer us away from the eruptions.

Above my head, a camera zipped down from the ceiling and pivoted toward me.

"Kyrion . . ." Roderick's singsong voice boomed out of the device. "Oh, Kyrion . . . Where are you . . ."

My hands clenched into fists, and I had to swallow another snarl. He knew *exactly* where I was. Taunting people was just another part of Roderick's sick little hunting game, and I wasn't going to give him the satisfaction of responding.

I stalked down one walkway after another, searching for something I could use as a weapon, but there was nothing here but lava. I considered backtracking and trying to find another biodome, but sooner or later, Roderick would get tired of chasing me, and either he or Jeffrey would start triggering traps to try to take me down. Better to make a stand here and now.

Another bubble of lava popped in one of the cauldrons, drawing my attention. The longer I stared at the lava, the more Vesper's seer magic surged and outlined it in a bright silver glow. I frowned. I didn't need Vesper's ability to know the lava was dangerous. Or was there another reason her power had pointed it out?

The glow of Vesper's power faded away, but my mind started churning. Perhaps I was looking at the situation the wrong way. I'd wanted to put some obstacles in Roderick's path. Well, there was no greater, deadlier obstacle than lava. Perhaps it was time to turn Roderick's own maze against him.

A hasty plan formed in my mind, and I strode into the gladiator ring in the middle of the biodome. Then I turned around and waited for my enemy.

Less than two minutes later, Roderick strutted into the Magma biodome still wearing his armor and carrying his war hammer.

The lunarium weapon was now glowing a bright, vivid red, mirroring the color of the lava. I ground my teeth to hold back another shudder.

Roderick strode forward and stopped several feet away. "Hello, Kyrion," he said, throwing his arms out wide. "You finally found the Magma biodome. Isn't it ingenious?"

"Your House really must have credits to burn if you can afford to keep pools of lava bubbling away in here," I snarked.

He dropped his arms and shrugged. "My family has several factories on Magma planets. Harnessing the lava is easier than you might think. I'm sure Vesper would admire the science behind it. She's an engineer, right?"

My hands clenched into fists. He knew good and well Vesper was an engineer.

"Nothing to say?" Roderick chuckled. "Pity. I always like to have a conversation with my special guests before the end."

The holoscreen on his left forearm lit up, and a sharp crackle of static sounded.

"Sir, we have a problem." Jeffrey's apologetic voice echoed out of the device. "I've lost the woman. Repeat. I've lost the woman."

Roderick frowned, although he kept his gaze on me. "What do you mean, you've lost the woman?"

There was a moment's silence, then Jeffrey cleared his throat. "She incapacitated the Black Scarab and disabled the camera I was using to track her, along with her holocuff."

"Well, find her," Roderick snapped, an irritated note creeping into his voice. "And when you locate her, seal her in one of the sections. I'll deal with her later."

Jeffrey cleared his throat again. "I'm not certain she's still in the maze, sir."

Roderick blinked and blinked, as though it had never occurred to him that someone could escape his hunting ground.

"I've switched the cameras to thermal imaging, but I'm not

seeing her body heat anywhere in the maze," Jeffrey replied. "I think she . . . got out."

Hope welled up in my chest. I reached out through the bond, just in case this was a cruel psychological trick, but the ribbon of Vesper had stretched out even further, and even more determination was rippling off her. I let out a soft, relieved laugh, and my inner monster purred with satisfaction. I'd been right. Vesper *had* escaped from the maze.

Roderick glared at me like it was my fault Vesper had wriggled out of his trap. "How did she get out?"

"I ran a diagnostic scan," Jeffrey replied. "Looks like she found an emergency control and used it to manually open an exit in the exterior wall."

Roderick's lips mashed together into a thin angry line, and a muscle tic-tic-ticced in his jaw like a timer counting down to an explosion. "Well, *find* her," he growled. "Right now. Or I'll be hunting *you* in here next. Understand?"

"Yes, sir," Jeffrey replied in a low, strained voice.

The holoscreen let out another crackle of static, and the light winked out.

This time, I was the one who clucked my tongue in mock sympathy. "Your technician underestimating Vesper is going to be the death of you, Roddy. Vesper is much more dangerous with her seer magic than you are with all your toys, tricks, and traps."

An angry flush swept up Roderick's neck and flooded his cheeks, turning them the same bloodred as his armor. "My Hammers will find Vesper and put her right back in the maze. Why, I might even have time to have a little fun with Vesper before we ship her out."

Ship her out? To where? And to whom? Was someone helping the Erzton lord with his house of horrors? If so, what did they want with Vesper?

Roderick shook his head, flinging off his anger like a dog

shedding water from its coat. The flush faded from his cheeks, and when he focused on me again, he was calm. "I love that look on your face."

"What *look*?" I asked in a wary voice.

He grinned, his white teeth gleaming in his mouth. "When the prey finally realizes they're caught in my trap and there is no escape."

Roderick tightened his grip on his hammer and strode forward. I grabbed my psion power and watched him approach. As soon as Roderick passed the first pool of lava, I snapped up my right hand and lashed out with my telekinesis.

Usually, when I picked up an object with my psion power, I sensed the general weight and heft of it, if not always the tactile sensation or the actual temperature of the rock, branch, or whatever item I was tossing at an enemy. I had never tried to move lava before, and as soon as I touched it with my telekinesis, a burning sensation erupted in my hand, like I was trying to throw lumps of red-hot mud that kept slipping through my fingers.

Sweat poured down my face, but I snarled and tightened my grip on my telekinesis, and a ball of lava floated up out of the pool—

A hidden door opened in one of the walls, and a metal nozzle jutted out and swiveled toward me.

Pew!

A blaster bolt zinged through the air. I spun in that direction. My right hand was already busy holding the lava, so I flung my left hand out, trying to use my telekinesis to redirect the bolt just as I had done earlier to the jets of water in the Frozon biodome.

But I was too slow and too distracted by the lava, and the bright orange-red streak of electricity punched straight into my palm. I screamed and staggered back, clutching my left hand to my chest. I also lost my grip on my telekinesis, and the lumpy ball of lava splattered back down into the pool.

Hot, electric agony clawed past my wrist and chewed a path all the way up to my elbow. My entire arm was twitching from the pulsing pain, but I looked down and forced my trembling fingers to open. A deep, gruesome blaster burn covered my palm, as though it was a cut of meat that was red, rare, and bloody around the edges and charred to a blackened crisp in the center.

I gritted my teeth and threw up another psionic shield, walling off this fresh injury. I hissed out a breath as some of the intense, pulsing pain receded, but I couldn't use my left hand, not even to pick up anything with my telekinesis. The slightest physical weight or psionic strain would crack my mental shield and flood my body with crippling pain.

"Poor Kyrion," Roderick drawled. "Such a rookie mistake. You aren't the first psion to try to use the Magma biodome against me. Did you really think I would let you throw lava at me?"

I swallowed another scream. Sweat streamed down my face, nausea roiled in my stomach, and it was all I could do not to vomit. Just looking at my scorched palm made the pain flare up even brighter and hotter and batter against my psionic shield, so I dropped my left hand to my side and tried to forget it was attached to the rest of my body.

Roderick laughed at my obvious distress. "Let me guess. Your hand feels like it is on fire, and your injury is hurting much worse than a typical blaster burn. Jeffrey came up with the ingenious idea to combine the lava with the blaster traps. I don't really understand how it works, but it is quite effective and extremely painful. As you can feel for yourself."

I was still too busy trying not to vomit to respond.

Roderick studied me a moment longer, then nodded, like he'd come to an important decision. "As much fun as this has been, Kyrion, I am on a bit of a schedule. I think we've played the game long enough. Besides, the grand finale is always my favorite part."

He grinned again, then started swinging his hammer back and forth, slicing it through the air with ease as he approached me with all the confidence of a king marching toward a conquered land.

A chilling realization swept over me, icing out some of the agonizing pain in my hand. I was well and truly caught, like a Frozon wolf in a snare, with no hope of escaping the death that was quickly approaching me.

FIFTEEN

VESPER

I slid the detonator into my pants pocket, then stuffed the larger box of explosives into a cloth bag that was lying on a counter. I also made sure the dead Hammer's blaster was set to its full, killing power, instead of stun. I slid the weapon onto my belt and grabbed my trusty trident again.

With the bag in one hand and my trident in the other, I left the transport garage and quickly returned to the upper level. I peered down the main corridor, just as I had a few minutes ago.

Everything was the same in the control room. Jeffrey was still at the panel, swiping through screens and trying to locate me, while holograms of Kyrion and Roderick flickered in the air. Asterin and Siya were still shackled to the table in the back and being guarded by four House Battis Hammers. The warriors looked bored, but Asterin and Siya kept glancing at each other, having a whispered telepathic conversation I couldn't hear.

First things first, I had to get the Hammers away from my friends. Once Asterin and Siya were safe, then I could deal with

Jeffrey, take his place at the control panel, and figure out where Kyrion was in the maze.

Jeffrey froze, and his eyes widened, like he'd just had a startling revelation. He leaned forward, frantically typing on a holoscreen. Something beeped in response, and the technician let out a low, muttered curse.

"What is it?" one of the male Hammers asked. "What's wrong?"

"Shut up and let me think," Jeffrey snarled.

The technician paced back and forth in front of the control panel for the better part of a minute. Then he sighed and flipped a switch, causing a bit of static to crackle through the air. Jeffrey wet his lips and leaned forward over the microphone sticking up out of the panel. "Sir, we have a problem. I've lost the woman . . ."

I stayed in my hiding spot and eavesdropped while Jeffrey told Roderick that I had escaped from the maze. I listened carefully, hoping to hear Kyrion talking in the background, but Roderick's pissed voice drowned out everything else.

Kyrion? I sent out the thought.

I still didn't hear his voice, but the sticky cobweb of him in my mind practically glowed with warm pride. Kyrion was happy I'd gotten out of the maze. Even more determination to save him roared through me.

Roderick ordered Jeffrey to find me. The technician agreed, then flipped the switch and turned off the microphone. He looked over his shoulder at the four Hammers and snapped his fingers at them. "You heard the boss. Find the woman. *Now*. And make sure you capture her. Roderick will take it out on all of us if you accidentally kill her and break the deal he's made."

My eyes narrowed. What deal? And what did it have to do with me?

"What about them?" one of the female Hammers asked, jerking her chin at Asterin and Siya.

"What about them?" Jeffrey scoffed. "They're shackled to

a table with psionic dampeners clamped around their wrists. They're no threat."

Asterin and Siya both glared at the technician. Then they looked at each other, once again having a whispered telepathic conversation. Asterin raised her eyebrows in a silent question, and Siya gave her a grim nod. Both women dropped their hands and gripped the edges of the table, their knuckles going white against their skin. My friends had a plan. Good. Me too.

"Go! Now!" Jeffrey made a shooing motion with his hand.

The four Hammers grumbled, but they left the control room and tromped along the corridor.

I tightened my grip on the trident and the bag containing the box of explosives. Then I drew in a breath and stepped out into the open where the other warriors could see me.

"Woo-woo." I let out a loud whistle.

The Hammers froze. Startled, Jeffrey looked up from the control panel, and Asterin and Siya also stared in my direction.

I shook the bag in my hand, and the black box of explosives slid out of the cloth and tumbled to the floor. I tossed the cloth aside, then stepped forward and kicked the box as hard as I could. It slid to a stop right in front of the four Hammers.

"BOOM!" I screamed, and charged forward.

The Hammers' eyes widened, and they all yelled, broke formation, and dove to opposite sides of the corridor, trying to get out of the blast radius, even though the box hadn't exploded.

But that was part of my plan. As much as I wanted to blow my enemies sky-high, I didn't know how powerful the explosives were, and I didn't want to obliterate myself, Asterin, and Siya. Besides, I needed Jeffrey alive and the control panel intact so I could help Kyrion.

I raced toward the two Hammers on the right, both of whom had thrown themselves down onto the floor and covered their heads with their hands, as if that would have saved them from anything.

The first Hammer lifted his head. "What the—"

I rammed the trident into his back. The Hammer screamed, his arms and legs flailed wildly, and he twisted to the side. I yanked the trident out of his body, then rammed it right back in again. The Hammer screamed a second time and kept flailing around, so I kicked him in the head. His screams cut off, and he slumped down to the floor.

Beside him, the second Hammer cursed and scrambled to her feet. I yanked the blaster off my belt and shot her in the chest.

Pew! Pew! Pew!

The woman shrieked and tumbled to the floor. Her war hammer fell out of her hand and slid to a stop at my feet.

Across the corridor, the remaining two warriors—a woman and a man—also cursed and got to their feet.

Since Kyrion was still in the maze and surrounded by psionic dampeners, the mental white fog was still wisping through my mind. I stretched through the haze and plunged my hands into the sticky cobweb of his presence. I grasped as many trickles of his telekinesis as I could, then used his power to sling the war hammer across the floor.

The woman easily sidestepped the skittering weapon, but the man stopped and lurched awkwardly to the side, coming closer to me.

Pew! Pew! Pew!

I also shot him in the chest with the blaster, and he screamed and dropped to the floor.

The woman growled and charged forward, lashing out with her own hammer. I ducked her first blow but not the second one, and she slammed the flat side of the weapon into my stomach.

"Oof!" The hard, bruising blow punched the air out of my lungs and tossed me back.

I bounced off the wall and staggered forward. The trident

slipped through my fingers and tumbled end over end down the corridor. I lifted the blaster in my other hand, but the woman spun her hammer around and knocked the weapon out of my grasp. Then she charged forward, put her shoulder down, and shoved me against the wall. She drew her hammer back, then swung it toward my chest. I reached out and locked my hands around her forearms, stopping her strike.

The woman snarled. I did too, and we seesawed back and forth, with her trying to drive the sharp spike on one side of her hammer into my chest and me desperately trying to hold her off.

"Alive!" Jeffrey yelled. "We need her alive!"

But the Hammer wasn't interested in keeping me alive. Not after I'd just killed three of her friends. She snarled again, dug her feet into the floor, and leaned forward, once again trying to drive the spike into my chest.

I braced my body against the wall and pushed back, but the Hammer was stronger than me, and it was only a matter of time before she shoved past my defenses. I needed a new plan right now.

As if she had heard my thoughts, the woman snarled and surged forward again . . . and this time I let her.

I released her arms and jerked out of the way. The woman yelped, surprised by the sudden lack of resistance, and her own momentum propelled her into the wall.

Bang!

The spike on the hammer punched into the wall right where my heart had been. The woman grunted and tried to yank the weapon free, but she'd put all her strength into the blow, and the hammer was deeply wedged in the concrete.

I scrambled around her, flung my hand out toward the blaster I'd dropped earlier, and reached for Kyrion's telekinesis. Once again, I could only access trickles of his power. Instead of spinning through the air, the blaster merely skipped along the floor. Frustration pounded through me.

The Hammer finally wrenched her weapon free, spun around, and stormed toward me. She clutched the hilt with both hands and raised the hammer high, ready to bring it down and crack my head open like a walnut. I stretched my fingers out a little farther and grabbed a few more trickles of Kyrion's power . . .

The blaster finally lifted off the ground and floated toward me. I stepped forward and scooped it up. The instant the weapon settled into my hand, I whirled to the side and fired.

Pew! Pew! Pew!

The bright red bolts slammed into the woman's chest, knocking her back against the wall. Her body slumped to the floor, and the war hammer slipped out of her hands and tumbled away.

I stood there, breathing hard, my finger still curled around the trigger in case any of the four warriors weren't as dead as I thought—

A small squeak sounded. I whirled in that direction.

Behind the control panel, Jeffrey let out another squeak of shock. I ran toward him, still clutching the blaster.

Jeffrey's eyes widened. He lunged toward the panel, his fingers flying over the buttons. I kept running. I had to reach him before he activated some self-defense mechanism.

With a collective roar, Asterin and Siya lifted the table they were cuffed to off the ground, churned their legs, and surged forward.

Jeffrey spun toward them. He tried to dart out of the way, but his red jacket snagged on a switch sticking out of the control panel, pinning him in place.

Asterin and Siya roared again and rammed the table into his stomach, practically folding the technician in half. Jeffrey let out a high-pitched scream, although the noise rapidly trailed off into a raspy gurgle.

Asterin and Siya shuffled back, still holding the table between them, and set it down. I sprinted into the control room and aimed my blaster at Jeffrey, but his eyes rolled up into the back of his head, and he toppled to the floor.

"It's about time you got here," Asterin said. "I thought Siya and I were going to have to rescue ourselves."

I grinned at my friend's dark humor. "Looks to me like the two of you were doing a pretty good job of it. Now, hold still and turn your head away."

Asterin did as I asked, and I used the blaster to shoot her chain free from the table. Then I went around and did the same thing to Siya's chain.

"Thanks for the assist, Vesper." Siya nodded at me.

I lifted the blaster to my forehead in a mock salute. "Anytime."

Still wearing the cuffs, Siya jogged past me and headed out into the hallway. She crouched down and rifled through the pockets of a dead Hammer's jacket. She let out a cry of triumph and pulled out a set of keys, which she used to open the cuffs on her wrists.

Siya jogged back into the control room with the key and opened Asterin's cuffs.

"What happened?" I asked.

"We were watching the holograms of you and Kyrion when the four Hammers came into the control room," Siya replied. "They claimed they wanted to watch you two go through the maze since Kyrion was an Arrow, so we all gathered around the table. The second Asterin and I turned our backs, the Hammers overpowered us, took our weapons, and slapped cuffs on our wrists." Her nostrils flared with disgust. "Roderick didn't even have the balls to come here and fight us himself."

Asterin flinched at the venom in Siya's voice, but she didn't chime in.

"And then?" I asked.

"And then Jeffrey sicced that Black Scarab on you and gave

Roderick the all clear to enter the maze and start hunting Kyrion," Siya replied. "You know the rest."

I went over and crouched down beside Jeffrey. The technician's eyes were closed, but his chest moved up and down in a steady rhythm. I slapped him across the face a few times, just in case he was faking, but he was out cold.

Frustration surged through me, but I stepped over Jeffrey and took his place at the control panel. Two holograms hovered in the air—Roderick, in his red armor, and Kyrion, who bore a small black X on his right forearm, the same spot where I'd felt that telltale sting earlier. But the injury didn't seem to be bothering Kyrion, who was facing off with Roderick.

The hologram of Kyrion waved his hand, using his telekinesis to lift some object I couldn't see. An instant later, a blaster bolt streaked through the air toward him.

"No!" I yelled, and flung my hand out, as though I could stop the bolt, even though I wasn't in the maze.

The sticky cobweb of Kyrion exploded with pain. A white-hot spike rammed through my left hand, and I hissed and recoiled in shock. In an instant, my skin turned a bright, vivid red like I had just grabbed a steaming brewmaker with my bare hand. The pain of the injury throbbed through my entire body, keeping time to the frantic, worried beat of my heart. If the injury was this painful for me, it must be devastating for Kyrion.

I gritted my teeth and ignored the psionic echoes of Kyrion's pain as best I could. I focused on the control panel again, looking at the embedded holoscreens and the knobs and levers. I started to hit a blue button, then abruptly stopped. I didn't know what the button controlled, and I might unleash some trap or obstacle that would further injure Kyrion.

I growled with frustration and paced back and forth in front of the control panel. I stopped long enough to kick Jeffrey in the ribs, but the technician remained unconscious.

Siya scooped up her war hammer from a table in the back,

and the lunarium weapon lit up with the bright green flare of her magic.

"Now what?" Asterin asked, grabbing a small silver blaster from the same table.

Siya twirled her hammer around in her hand. "Now we see if any more of these bastards are in the facility." She looked at me and frowned. "Vesper? Why aren't you taking control of the maze?"

Anger and frustration simmered through my veins. "Because I can't figure out what all these blasted buttons do, and I don't want to hit the wrong one and make things worse for Kyrion."

My anger drained away, replaced by a cold fist of dread that squeezed my heart. "I have to get back to the maze. I have to help Kyrion."

I moved away from the panel, but Siya stepped forward, blocking my path.

"You'll never make it in time," she said, her voice not unkind. "The maze is huge, and Kyrion went in on the far side of the facility."

Asterin nodded. "Siya is right. We'll clear this level, then head down to the maze. You stay here and keep working on the controls. You can figure it out, Vesper. I know you can."

"Me too," Siya chimed in.

My friends stared at me, and the belief shining in their eyes made the fist of dread loosen around my heart. I blew out a breath and nodded at them.

"Okay, you two make sure there are no more Hammers lurking around. I'll try to reach Kyrion through the control panel. Maybe I can figure out how to guide him away from Roderick or at least put some obstacles between them."

Weapons in their hands, Siya and Asterin ran out of the room.

I kicked Jeffrey in the ribs again, but the technician remained limp and unconscious. I growled and stalked back over to the control panel.

"Okay, Vesper," I muttered. "You can figure this out. It's just like any control panel in the R&D lab. Just focus on one thing at a time."

I drew in a deep breath, filling my lungs with air, then whooshed it out. I had an oxygen optimization, or O2, enhancement, which meant that a special liquid had been injected into my lungs that dramatically increased their capacity and functionality. To me, breathing in and out had a great soothing effect, and the simple action of holding and releasing my breath worked its magic yet again.

Calmer, I leaned down and peered at the buttons. A few were labeled with words like *fog* and *water*, but I had no idea where they were in the maze or how large—or dangerous—an element they might create. I could push all the buttons I wanted, but if I didn't affect the environment around Kyrion, then I wouldn't help him at all.

Instead of hitting a button, I waved my hand over the holoscreens embedded in the panel. The screens flared with light, but they didn't project any new images up into the air. The figures of Kyrion and Roderick were still flickering over one screen, but I didn't get a sense of their location, and I couldn't figure out how to pull up a map. In its own way, the control panel was also a maze, and I was running out of time to navigate it.

I slapped the edge of the panel in frustration, making the lights blink, as though they were chiding me for treating them so harshly. The holograms of Kyrion and Roderick also flickered again. The motion reminded me of the memories that filled the doors in my mindscape. A growl escaped my lips. Right now, I needed to see what Kyrion was seeing, not a memory from my past or a vision of a possible future—

Wait. Why *couldn't* I see what Kyrion was seeing? I'd been so focused on trying to use his telepathy and telekinesis that I hadn't considered how my *own* abilities might be useful in this situation. In the maze, I'd used my seer magic to spot the broken lizard statue and the trident and turn them into weapons. Now I just needed to do the same thing to myself.

I chewed my lower lip, my mind whirring. A few weeks ago, I'd walked through a door in my mindscape and astrally projected myself into Zane's library at Castle Zimmer, even though I had never been there before in real life. Why couldn't I do the same thing again now?

Maybe the answer to helping Kyrion wasn't a button on the control panel. Maybe it was my own magic.

As soon as the idea popped into my mind, I could see how it might—*might*—work. Aldrich and Verona Collier had sent us to the training facility to deepen and strengthen our truebond, but part of that included Kyrion and me learning more about our own individual powers and how they might complement our respective psionic abilities.

"Bond of two," I whispered. "Tried and true."

Asterin had told Kyrion and me to use that code phrase if we ever needed help from the Hammers, but now I could see the deeper meaning in the words.

I blew out another breath and braced my hands on the edge of the control panel. Then I closed my eyes and reached for my seer power.

It was time to put my own magic to the test.

For a moment, everything was black. Then light bloomed, and I found myself in the corridor of an old-fashioned castle—Castle Caldaren, Kyrion's home on Corios. Normally, I would have taken a moment to admire the fine furnishings, but Kyrion was running out of time, so I sprinted past the tables and chairs made of real wood, stone, and glass.

My boots smacked out a soft rhythm on the plush rugs. I careened around a grandfather clock and sprinted into a library filled with shelves of real paper books. A silver-framed portrait of a young Kyrion and his parents hung over the fireplace, and Desdemona Caldaren turned her head and smiled at me the way she always did whenever I came in here.

I moved past the Regal lady and waved my hand. A door appeared in the wall close to the fireplace and flung itself open, and I charged through to the other side.

A familiar set of spiral stairs appeared. I leaped down the stone steps two and three at a time, keeping my right hand on the railing for balance. At my touch, sigils lit up one after another along the length of the railing, but I ignored the mammoth butterflies flapping their wings and the stormswords crackling with fire, ice, lightning, and wind.

I leaped off the bottom step and sprinted into an enormous round room. Blue-moon peonies bobbed up and down on long black vines that crawled up and draped over the doors set into the dark gray stone wall. Wide, open, unblinking sapphsidian eyes were embedded in many of the doors, and the jewels winked and glimmered with light, almost as if they approved of my frantic pace.

I raced past several doors. Some were open, and memories played on the other side like videos on holoscreens.

Useless child . . . My mother, Nerezza, sneered from one doorway, while Esmina Reston gloated at me from another one. *You're the weak link, destined to be broken* . . .

For once, I moved past the hurtful memories without stopping, and I kept running until I came to three doors in the back of the room. The fancy, curlicued *Z* of House Zimmer marked one as Zane's door, while a large upside-down sapphsidian eye adorned another door. The Door, as I always thought of it, led into the dark, distant depths of my mindscape where my psionic nexus was located.

I focused on the third door, where the House Caldaren sigil arrow streaked upward through a cluster of stars. I had never tried to open Kyrion's door before. Just because we were bonded didn't mean I had the right to rifle through Kyrion's thoughts, feelings, and memories like they were playing cards in a game. I respected his privacy far too much for that.

But right now, I was more interested in saving his life, so I waved my hand. To my surprise, the sapphsidian arrow glimmered brightly, as did the carvings of the surrounding stars, and the door cracked open. I hesitated, then waved my hand again. The door swung all the way open, like Kyrion himself was inviting me inside. I swallowed a hard knot of worry in my throat, drew in another breath, and charged through to the other side.

A few weeks ago, when I had stepped through Zane's door, it had been like crossing a threshold and moving from one room to another. Simple, quick, and easy.

Maybe it was due to the psionic dampeners still muting our connection, but stepping through Kyrion's door was like falling into a distant dream. Strange, slow, and awkward.

Everything went black, and I had the sensation of streaking downward like a shooting star dropping from the sky and about to slam into the earth . . .

My entire body jolted, and my eyes snapped open. For a moment, everything remained dark, and then light bloomed, just as it had when I'd first entered my mindscape.

I blinked, and from one moment to the next, everything snapped into focus. Flagstones underfoot, a circular metal wall, a clear energy shield shimmering overhead. I had done it. I had astrally projected myself into the maze.

Triumph pulsed through me, but it quickly wilted away as I took in an unexpected but nauseatingly familiar feature. Permaglass pools and bronze cauldrons were scattered throughout the area, and every single container was filled with lava.

This biodome was fashioned after a Magma planet.

Even though my physical body wasn't actually in the biodome, the intense, oppressive heat still blasted over me and sucked the moisture out of my body. An unexpected and unwelcome side effect of my seer magic. The sensation stirred up memories of the Techwave battle on Magma 7, but I pushed them aside. I didn't have time for memories right now—only rogue actions.

Kyrion was standing off to my left. His black hair was plastered to his forehead, and his skin was red and chapped. Sweat trickled down his face and spattered onto his dark blue clothes, and dust coated his knee-high boots.

An ugly burn from a blaster bolt marred Kyrion's right forearm, but that was a minor injury compared with his left hand, which looked like he'd stuck it into the lava. His palm was as black as charcoal, and his fingers were a bright, unnatural red and twisted at an awkward angle like he couldn't move them.

Just looking at Kyrion's injuries made the pain of them flare up in my own body again. My left hand spasmed, and I couldn't stop my fingers from curving into the same awkward claw as Kyrion's fingers. A couple of weeks ago, I'd been shot with a powerful blaster when some bounty hunters had cornered me on Tropics 44, but the sheer, unrelenting agony pulsing off Kyrion took my breath away. I didn't see how the Arrow was still on his feet, much less glaring at Roderick like he wanted to rip the other warrior to pieces with his bare hands.

If walking through Kyrion's door had been like entering a distant dream, then Roderick was the nightmare that was front and center. His red armor was even brighter and shinier than the pools of lava, making him seem like he was wearing polyplastic plates of blood. Disgust curdled in my stomach.

Sweat kept dripping down Kyrion's face, but not a single drop appeared on Roderick's forehead, and his skin wasn't flushed. His armor must be equipped with a cooling and heating system that adjusted to the surrounding environment and temperature. I snorted. Of course it was. The Erzton lord wouldn't want to be the least bit uncomfortable as he hunted people.

Being in the maze and seeing the area from this angle made it much easier to orient myself, but I still wanted—*needed*—more information, so I called up my seer magic and studied the rest of the biodome. I concentrated on the bronze cauldrons and the metal wall, since those were the most likely places for hidden traps. My magic kicked in and highlighted a few nozzles and other hazards, and I marked those spots in the mental map I was creating.

My body trembled, and sweat streamed down my face, although I thought my physical distress had more to do with using my magic in such a focused, prolonged way than with the intense, almost unbearable heat of the lava.

I blinked, and everything wavered, as though it was a mirage. I clenched my hands into fists and gripped my seer magic a little more tightly, along with the sticky cobweb of Kyrion. Slowly, everything solidified.

I reached for more of my magic, anchoring myself to it, along with this spot in the maze. I only had one shot at this, and I had to make it work—or Kyrion was dead.

In my mind's eye, I was still in the biodome watching Kyrion and Roderick face off. Keeping that image front and center in my thoughts, I slowly cracked my eyes open back out in the real world.

The control panel with its plethora of buttons and blinking lights swam into view. I curled my right hand around the metal. The sharp edge pressed into my palm, grounding me back in the control room, even as the image of Kyrion and Roderick flickered in my mind, like a holoscreen about to go dark. I ground my teeth and tightened my grip on my seer power and the sticky cobweb of Kyrion yet again.

The real-world view of the control panel warred with the image of the maze in my mind, like I was trying to watch two different gossipcasts at the same time. I thought my brain was going to explode from the intense pressure, but I reached for even more of my magic, and both images slowly steadied.

I drew in a breath, then let it out. When I was certain I had a good grip on my magic and especially my connection to Kyrion, I flexed my fingers, leaned over the control panel, and started hitting buttons.

SIXTEEN

KYRION

Roderick stopped and stared at me, like I was a cherished photo he was committing to memory. No doubt the arrogant lord wanted to remember every second of his wretched hunt.

Then he grinned and advanced toward me, swinging his hammer back and forth. The lunarium weapon shimmered a darker, bloodier red than before, mirroring both his psion power and his sick anticipation of finishing his game.

A bright silver light flared, and a second version of Roderick appeared. I tensed, wondering if it was a hologram, a trick to get me to lower my guard, but then I realized it was Vesper's seer magic surging for some unknown reason. The light flared again, and a second version of myself appeared. My mirror image threw himself at Roderick, who lashed out with his hammer.

Crack! Crack! Crack!

Even though it was just a vision, I still heard the gruesome sounds of my ribs cracking, and phantom pain stabbed through my chest, stealing my breath.

The second Roderick grinned and lashed out with his hammer again, shoving my mirror image into one of the nearby glass pools. Horrified, I watched the lava close over my mirror image, who screamed and screamed as he was quickly incinerated . . .

I ground my teeth and shoved Vesper's power away. The silver light vanished, as did the image of my scalded skin, but an intense burning sensation cascaded through my body, and my own hoarse screams echoed in my ears. A fresh river of sweat streamed down my face, and even more nausea roiled in my gut. Fuck, that had been intense.

I might not know much about seer magic, but Vesper's power had clearly shown me a vision of the future. If I stayed where I was, I would be trapped in the gladiator-style ring in the center of the biodome. I would put up a vicious fight, but Roderick would eventually use his hammer to knock me into one of the pools, and the lava would end me.

A snarl rose in my throat, and my inner monster roared with rage. I wasn't going to die that easily. Not when Vesper would feel every agonizing second of my demise through our bond. I might not escape Roderick, but I would spare Vesper the gruesome shock of drowning in a pool of lava.

Despite the pain still pulsing through my ruined left hand and battering against the psionic shield in my mind, I snarled again and sprinted forward. Roderick also sprinted forward, trying to cut me off and force me back into the ring, but I sidestepped him.

Roderick spun toward me and lashed out with his hammer. He landed a solid blow on my left shoulder. Pain erupted in the joint, zinged down my arm, and merged with the agony still pulsing through my charred hand. I staggered to the side and almost plowed into a cauldron of lava before I finally managed to right myself. I threw up another psionic shield in my mind, walling off as much of the pain as possible, and kept going.

I ran toward the edge of the biodome. My gaze snapped left and right. I still needed a weapon, although I didn't see anything useful in here.

Another bright flare of silver caught my eye, and I was stunned to see Vesper standing in the biodome, regarding the pools of lava with a disgusted expression.

I skidded to a halt. *Vesper?*

I didn't really expect her to respond, since we hadn't been able to communicate clearly since entering the maze, but to my surprise, Vesper turned her head and looked straight at me. Blood covered her dark blue clothes and her hands. More blood speckled her face, and the silver flecks in her dark blue eyes glittered like distant stars.

A fist of fear crushed my heart. Was Vesper dead? Was this some final vision of her?

The flecks in her eyes grew larger and larger, as though two pools of shimmering liquid silver had been set into her face. The velvety ribbon of Vesper thrummed and vibrated with psion power, and a crackling sensation swept over my skin, like I was about to get a violent static shock.

I'm here, Kyr.

At the sound of her voice in my mind, my connection to Vesper snapped back into place, despite the psionic dampeners in the maze. The cold, tight fist of fear squeezing my chest vanished, and the ribbon of her quickly spooled back into its usual shape and size and curled snugly around my heart.

For a moment, I wondered how I was hearing and seeing Vesper, but then the answer came to me. She was tapping into her seer magic and astrally projecting herself into the maze just as she had once done in Zane's library. Clever, clever seer.

Vesper's gaze flicked past me and landed on Roderick, who was swinging his hammer back and forth and slowly approaching me again. *I'm going to help you kill him.*

How? He's wearing armor, and the biodome is rigged with

booby traps he can control through the holoscreen on his forearm.

Her eyes narrowed, and her lips puckered in thought. *I'm still figuring that out. Do me a favor, and stay away from the wall and the lava, okay?*

Another bubble of lava popped in a cauldron beside my left elbow. I shuddered. *Not a problem.*

Vesper glanced around the biodome. Her eyes narrowed, and her brow furrowed as she analyzed and cataloged one thing after another. I'd seen that same look on her face whenever she was building a makeshift weapon on board the *Dream World*. My inner monster rumbled with satisfaction and pride. Vesper's thinking face was one of my favorite expressions.

Roderick stopped, frowned, and looked at the spot where Vesper was standing. "What are you staring at with that stupid smile on your face?"

As difficult as it was, I pulled my gaze away from Vesper and focused on him again. "Your death."

Roderick snorted. "The heat has already addled your mind. Or perhaps the nasty blaster burn on your hand is making it hard for you to think clearly. The only person who's dying is you, Kyrion."

I didn't bother responding. Vesper Quill was better at figuring out how things worked than anyone else in the entire galaxy, and she would come up with a way for me to defeat Roderick.

The bastard was already dead. He just didn't know it yet.

Roderick's eyes narrowed in suspicion. "It's your truebond, isn't it? You're talking to your precious Vesper. Somehow she escaped the maze and moved far enough away from the psionic dampeners to communicate with you. Well, she won't get far. My people have strict orders not to let anyone leave the facility." A cruel grin twisted his lips. "Not alive, anyway."

I killed the four Hammers guarding the control room,

Vesper's voice sounded in my mind, and her image wavered like a ghost coming into and out of focus. *Siya and Asterin are clearing the rest of the facility right now.*

I focused on Roderick again. "You should have done more research on Vesper. Then you would have known not to underestimate her. The people you left behind in the control room are dead, and I'm willing to bet Siya and Asterin are calling in reinforcements from House Collier even as we speak."

For the first time, a bit of uncertainty creased Roderick's face, but it quickly vanished, swallowed by his enormous ego. "You're bluffing. Vesper might have gotten lucky and slipped out of the maze, but there's no way she could have infiltrated the control room without getting captured."

I jerked my chin at the holoscreen on his left forearm. "Go ahead. Check for yourself."

Roderick wet his lips, then lifted the holoscreen. "Jeffrey, what's your status?"

Silence.

"Jeffrey, what's your status?" Roderick repeated, his voice even sharper than before. "Report. *Now*."

The holoscreen flared with light, and Roderick exhaled with relief.

"Jeffrey is indisposed." Vesper's voice sounded through the device. "Siya and Asterin rammed a table into him. Poor Jeffrey is currently sleeping off a concussion and a couple of cracked ribs."

Roderick recoiled in shock, although he quickly lifted the screen back to his lips. "Pierre, report," he commanded in a low, urgent voice. "Nasir. Eden. Macie."

"I'm assuming those are the four Hammers you left in the control room to subdue Siya and Asterin." Once again, Vesper's voice crackled through the device. "I stabbed one of them with a trident that I took off a mermaid statue in the maze, then shot the other three with a blaster."

"Iker, report," Roderick barked into the screen.

"If that's the guy in the transport garage, then he's dead too," Vesper replied in a cheerful voice. "Another death by trident. I also grabbed the box of explosives he was going to plant on the House Collier transport so you could blow up Siya's ship and make our deaths look like an accident. I haven't decided what I'm going to do with the explosives yet, but I'm sure I'll think of *something*."

I grinned. *Now you're just bragging, seer.*

She grinned back at me. *Absolutely, Arrow.*

Vesper looked over at Roderick. "Oh, and just in case you were wondering, I also locked you out of the main control panel." Once again, her voice floated out of the holoscreen on his forearm. "Which means I'm in full command of the maze now, along with all its hazards and booby traps."

Roderick angrily stabbed the holoscreen a few times with his right index finger, but it didn't respond to his commands. He stared at the device in disbelief for a few seconds, then shook his head, as though flinging off the dregs of a bad dream. "It doesn't matter what you do, Vesper. I'm still here with Kyrion, and once I kill him and shatter your truebond, you'll *wish* you were dead."

Vesper's voice didn't sound through the holoscreen again, but the flickering image of her glared at Roderick with a murderous expression that made my inner monster rumble in satisfaction.

"Nothing to say?" Roderick called out in a mocking voice. "I thought not."

Another cruel smile twisted his face, and the other warrior moved toward me, once again swinging his hammer from side to side. With every step he took, more psion power sparked to life and crackled around the lunarium weapon. His rage also scraped against my telempathy, burning just as hot as the bubbling lava around us.

Hold still, Vesper's voice sounded in my mind.

I did as she asked. Roderick's steps quickened. He growled and raised his hammer high, and psion power spit, hissed, and crackled around the weapon like crimson lightning. The warrior leaped forward and brought the hammer down, aiming for my chest, but I held my position, trusting Vesper to protect me.

Whoosh!

A jet of water spewed out from a hidden wall nozzle. The powerful blast hit Roderick in the side and knocked him back. He lost his balance, and for a moment, I thought he might careen into one of the cauldrons, but he dug his armored boots into the ground and steadied himself. Pity.

The water kept spraying, hitting the permaglass pools and bronze cauldrons. A crusty black film formed on some of the lava, partially solidifying it, while massive clouds of steam erupted from other spots, making the biodome even hotter.

The jet of water abruptly cut off, although steam kept hissing and rising in spots.

Drat, Vesper said. *I was hoping for a little more* oomph *than that.*

The velvety ribbon of her vibrated, and a series of *clicks*, *clanks*, and *clack-clack-clacks* sounded in my ears, like I was standing beside Vesper and watching her operate the main control panel.

Roderick snarled and whirled around. "It's going to take a lot more than a little water to kill me, Kyrion."

Once again, I didn't bother responding. Roderick still thought he was going to win, but he had lost the instant Vesper had taken control of the maze. The other warrior should have been trying to escape, not wasting time insulting me. Fool.

Roderick snarled, tightened his grip on his hammer, and headed toward me again.

Whoosh!

This time, instead of water, daggerlike chunks of ice shot out from a different nozzle. The chunks slammed into Roderick's chest and knocked him back again, although the ice quickly melted into nothingness.

Roderick growled and charged forward yet again. For the third time, I held my position.

Whoosh!

Flames shot out from yet another hidden nozzle. This blast was much wider and stronger than the water and the ice had been. The fire zipped right in front of Roderick, who yelped in surprise. He stumbled to the side, and his elbow clipped one of the cauldrons. A bubble of lava erupted straight into his face. Lava also sloshed out of the container and splattered onto his armor, and the acrid stench of melting polyplastic filled the air.

Roderick screamed and staggered away from the cauldron. I backed away from him, not wanting to get caught in a spray of lava.

Roderick whirled toward me. The left side of his face was horrifically burned, a patchwork of scalded red and charred black skin, and his red armor now featured several large smoldering black pits.

I raised my burned left hand and flashed my gnarled, twisted fingers at him. "Doesn't feel so good, does it?"

Roderick's dark brown eyes bulged with a combination of rage and pain. His hand tightened around the gold hilt of his war hammer, and he snarled and lunged forward.

I dodged the awkward blow, then spun around and snapped out my right hand. I used my telekinesis to pick up some of the cracked flagstones and hurled them at Roderick. Most of the chunks of stone harmlessly pelted his armor, but one soared up and slammed into the burned side of his face. Roderick's head jerked back at the sharp, smacking motion, and a high-pitched shriek erupted from his lips like he was a wounded animal.

Roderick whirled toward me, blood, tears, and snot streaming down his ruined face. He bared his teeth and stepped forward like he was going to attack me again . . .

And then he dropped the hammer to his side, spun around on his bootheel, and ran away.

I stood there, blinking, wondering if my eyes were playing tricks on me, but they weren't. Roderick was sprinting past the pools and cauldrons of lava and trying to get out of the Magma biodome as fast as possible.

He didn't want to kill me anymore. No, right now, the cheating, cowardly bastard was trying to escape and save his own skin.

My inner monster roared with rage. An answering snarl spewed from my throat, and I also sprinted past the lava.

Kyr, wait! Vesper's voice sounded in my mind. *If you go to another section of the maze, I'll lose track of you. I won't be able to trigger any more obstacles to help you. Kyr, wait!*

I don't need any more traps, I growled back. *He sicced a Black Scarab on you, and he's going to die for that.*

Frustration surged through the bond, and the image of Vesper threw her hands up in the air.

Renewed energy coursed through my body. My steps quickened, and I left the Magma biodome behind and plunged back into the maze.

The prey had just become the predator.

Despite his injuries, Roderick quickly outpaced me, thanks to the propulsion and other enhancements in his modified armor. I couldn't see him, although I could hear his footsteps clanking through the maze. Roderick had chosen speed over stealth, and he wasn't even trying to be quiet.

A junction loomed up ahead, but I couldn't tell which path he had taken.

Where is he? I called out through the bond. *Where did he go?*

Once again, a series of *clicks*, *clanks*, and *clack-clack-clacks* echoed in my ears. In the distance, a camera zoomed down from the ceiling and pivoted back and forth.

Right! Go right! Vesper's voice sounded in my mind, and the velvety ribbon of her thrummed in time to the rapid beat of my boots on the flagstones.

I veered onto that path. I still didn't see Roderick, but the clanking of his footsteps was a little louder.

Straight ahead, then take the next left! Vesper said.

Following her instructions, I plowed through the maze. I would have been hopelessly lost without Vesper tracking Roderick through the cameras, and the sound of her voice in my mind also helped me reinforce my psionic shields and block out the pain of my injuries. And most important of all, Vesper's determination mixed with my own through the bond and gave me fresh strength and energy.

Perhaps this was what Lord Aldrich and Lady Verona had wanted us to discover. That no matter how far apart Vesper and I were or how bruised and battered we might be, we could weather any storm, and we were always—*always*—stronger together.

Slow down! Vesper called out a warning. *I've lost track of Roderick. He went into the next biodome, but he must have turned off the sensors in his armor, because his hologram on the control panel vanished. I'm sorry, Kyr.*

That's okay. I'm more than happy to finish the job.

I did as she asked and slowed down, making my steps as soft and silent as possible. A few seconds later, the path curved, and the next biodome loomed into view. I stopped at the threshold.

This biodome was a Temperate forest filled with large trees, hedges, and shrubs sporting an array of autumn leaves, and the entire area was a riot of scarlet, gold, and blazing orange. Off to the side, a few large, fat pumpkins were clustered around a scarecrow in a red House Battis uniform that was slumped up against a short wooden stake like a dead body. Someone had used the scarecrow as target practice; its chest was adorned with blaster burns, and wads of singed straw had leaked out of its arms and legs.

Piles of fallen leaves covered the ground, hiding many of the paths, while still more leaves swirled through the air like jewel-toned snowflakes, thanks to a hidden wind machine. The floating, flying leaves made it hard to see much of anything, and the overhead lights had been positioned so that their rays sliced through the tree branches, creating a shadowy, dappled effect that further reduced visibility.

Roderick's red armor matched the color of many of the leaves, making the autumn forest biodome the perfect place for him to hide. I scanned the trees, hedges, and shrubs, but Roderick was staying still and blending in.

I didn't spot him, but I had another way to find my enemy. I reached out with my telempathy, and a presence pinged in my mind. One emotion after another wafted off Roderick—sharp worry, cold dread, and more than a little gut-churning fear.

The other warrior was brave when he had the advantage and things were going exactly according to plan, but now that his people were dead and Vesper was in control of the maze, he was on the verge of panicking. My inner monster licked its chops in anticipation.

This was going to be *fun*.

My telempathy might have revealed Roderick's presence, but it didn't tell me exactly where he was. I didn't just have my own psionic abilities to rely on, though—I also had Vesper's power.

I didn't often try to use Vesper's seer magic, as I never knew what awful memories or horrific futures it might show me. But right now, her power was the key to spotting my enemy, so I curled my fingers around the velvety ribbon of her in my mind.

In an instant, everything became brighter and more vivid. The brilliant colors and the tiny veins of the swirling leaves, the rough, knotted bark on the trees, even the thin bits of straw sticking out of the scarecrow like blackened needles. I could see all that and more, as though I was staring at my surroundings through a microscope in super-sharp focus. The visual bombardment made my brain pound and threatened to overwhelm me, but I curled my fingers a little more tightly around the velvety ribbon of Vesper like it was a life raft keeping me from being swept out into a churning sea of sensation.

My grip on her power steadied, and the world dimmed, like I had dialed back the color saturation on a hologram. My intense headache eased, and I exhaled with relief.

Still holding on to Vesper's seer magic, I reached out with my telempathy, once again focusing on Roderick's emotions, and I finally spotted the Erzton lord crouching behind a tree. I couldn't tell if he was planning to ambush me or hoping I would move on to another section of the maze so he could avoid me completely. It didn't matter either way. He wasn't leaving here alive.

Roderick might be panicking, but he still had a weapon, and I didn't, so I tightened my grip on Vesper's power and scanned the rest of the biodome. A bright silver flare appeared, drawing my gaze to the short, thick stake that was propping up the scarecrow. That would do quite nicely.

I studied Roderick a moment longer, as well as everything around him. Then I released Vesper's seer magic, along with my own telempathy, and spoke to her again.

I'm going to flush him out in the open. You make sure he can't escape the biodome.

You got it, Vesper replied.

I squared my shoulders and stepped through the energy shield. The maze itself was cool, but the air inside the Temperate biodome was cooler still, mimicking a crisp fall day. It would have been a pleasant place to train, but it was going to make an even better graveyard.

"Roderick . . ." I called out in the same annoying singsong tone he had used earlier. "Oh, Roderick . . . Where are you . . ."

My telempathy let me sense the exact moment the coward flinched.

I moved deeper into the biodome, my boots sending up sprays of leaves, twigs, and dirt. I followed a path that curved away from Roderick and headed toward the scarecrow display, although I kept peering at him out of the corners of my eyes. I stopped at the end of the path, like I was thinking about leaving the biodome and moving on to the next section.

The second I turned my back, he moved.

I whirled around. Instead of racing forward to attack me, Roderick was sprinting in the opposite direction, trying to escape the biodome and plunge back into the maze.

Whoosh!

A jet of water spewed out of a nozzle hidden in a tree trunk and slammed into Roderick's side. He grunted, but he kept going, still heading toward the exit.

Bzzt!

The energy shield that covered the biodome shimmered and started crackling with electricity. Roderick skidded to a halt right before he crossed the threshold. Pity. It would have been amusing to watch him slam into the shield and be zapped like a bug in his armored shell.

Roderick growled and slammed his hammer into the shield. More electricity crackled, and a shower of orange sparks fell over him, but the air kept shimmering, indicating the shield was still firmly in place.

"Vesper has control of the maze, remember?" I called out. "You can't escape me now."

Roderick growled again, then whirled around to face me. "You think you're such a great warrior," he hissed. "But I still have a suit of armor and a weapon, and you don't, Kyrion."

I crooked my right index finger at him in a clear challenge.

Roderick hesitated and glanced over his shoulder, as though he was thinking about whirling around and trying to force his way through the energy shield. That would have been the smart thing to do, despite the dangerous electrical charge that would shock and burn him to within an inch of his life, if not kill him outright.

Roderick looked at me. He hissed again, a bit of spittle flying out of his mouth like he was a rabid animal. Then he raised his hammer and charged at me.

This time, without the threat of bubbling lava all around, I was able to move freely. I easily sidestepped his blow, then used my telekinesis to wrench the stake I'd noticed earlier out of the ground. The scarecrow dropped away, and the stake zipped through the air and settled into my right hand.

A few splinters dug into my palm, but I ignored the discomfort and curled my fingers around the wood. The stake was a bit unwieldy, especially since I could only use it with my uninjured right hand, but it was heavy and substantial enough to do some damage.

Roderick spun around, reversed direction, and swung his hammer out in a vicious arc, trying to cave in my head with one deadly strike. I twisted to the side, avoiding the blow. He snarled and lifted his weapon again.

The instant Roderick raised the hammer over his head, I darted forward.

I didn't know if I had the physical strength to punch the stake through the lava-weakened spots in his armor, so I went low. With the help of my telekinesis, I used the chunk of wood like a short makeshift spear and drove the sharp, triangular point into the side of his right knee, which wasn't covered by an armored plate. I shoved the stake in as deep as I could, then yanked it out.

Roderick howled with pain. His right leg buckled, and he staggered away.

I chased after him and stabbed my makeshift spear into another exposed spot, the meaty area between the top of his left thigh and his hip. He howled with pain again, but he still didn't go down. I yanked the stake out, tightened my grip on the rough wood, and then drew it back like a shock baton and cracked it across his jaw.

Once again, I added my telekinesis to the blow, and I finally knocked Roderick down onto his back, which had been my goal all along. Just like that, I had the advantage.

Armor was great—if you were on your feet.

But the instant you went down, all that heavy protective armor became a serious liability. Instead of a tall, strong, imposing warrior, Roderick now looked like a giant red tortoise resting on its shell, and his arms and legs thrashed and flailed as he struggled to roll over onto his side.

I stepped up and kicked him in the face. Roderick's nose broke with a deeply satisfying crunch, and he blubbered as a fresh wave of blood, tears, and snot gushed down his burned face.

He swung his hammer out in a wild arc, trying to knock my feet out from under me, but I hopped over the weapon. I was still clutching the scarecrow stake, so I spun back around, dropped down, and stabbed the point into his right shoulder.

Roderick howled with pain. Blood welled up, and his hammer slipped out of his fingers. I straightened up and grabbed hold of his weapon with my telekinesis. The hammer zipped up through the air, and the gold hilt slapped against my right palm.

Roderick snarled, yanked the stake out of his shoulder, and lashed out with it, but I hopped over it as easily as I had his hammer a moment ago. Roderick dug the stake into the ground like a crutch. He grunted and finally heaved himself onto his hands and knees.

He flung the stake in my direction, then scuttled away from me like a crab streaking across a beach. I followed him, the war hammer still clutched in my hand. The lunarium was now glowing a dark, ominous blue and spitting out needles of ice in a reflection of my psion power, which was as strong as ever, thanks to my cold rage and icy determination.

Roderick crawled across the ground, heading toward a stone bench beneath one of the trees. He reached underneath the bench and yanked a small blaster out of a hiding spot. Then he spun toward me and aimed the weapon at my chest.

"Die, you bastard!" Roderick screamed, and pulled the trigger.

Pew!

Vesper's seer power kicked in just as it had done earlier in the Magma biodome. Time slowed down, and I noticed one thing after another. The bright orange streak of energy erupting out of the blaster. The crimson blood trickling down Roderick's face. The sharp tips of his white canines flashing like fangs in his mouth . . .

Time snapped back to its normal flow. I stepped up and used the lunarium head of the war hammer to deflect the bolt and send it shooting right back at Roderick.

Bull's-eye.

The bolt hit Roderick's armor in a spot close to his heart that had been scorched and softened by the lava, and the deadly blast of electricity punched right through the weakened polyplastic and tossed him back against the stone bench.

Roderick screamed. He tried to raise the blaster to fire again, but I kicked the weapon out of his hand. Roderick watched the blaster tumble end over end and sink into a pile of scarlet leaves.

His head slowly lifted. Weary resignation creased his burned face, and he looked up at me with dull eyes. Blood oozed out of the deep wound in his chest. The coppery tang mixed with the ozone stench of the bolt and created an unmistakable scent I had smelled countless times before.

The stench of impending death.

I loomed over him, the war hammer still clutched in my hand. "What did you say to me before? Ah, yes, now I remember. The grand finale is your favorite part. When the prey finally realizes they're caught in your trap and there is no escape." I nodded, and he flinched at the motion. "Finally, something we can agree on."

A humorless smile lifted Roderick's lips. "Looks like you are the better warrior after all, Kyrion . . ."

Roderick's voice trailed off, and his chest spasmed with a raspy, gurgling cough. He slumped a little more heavily against the bench, then slowly slid off the side and toppled over onto the ground. His eyes widened, then stilled. More blood leaked out of the wound in his chest, but it quickly ebbed, although the autumn leaves continued to swirl through the air.

The great hunter was dead, killed by the merciless monster he'd foolishly lured into his trap.

SEVENTEEN

VESPER

I twisted a knob on the control panel. In response, the camera hovering over the forest biodome lowered, giving me a better view through the swirling leaves.

Kyrion towered over Roderick, who was clearly dead. Good riddance. Kyrion exhaled and lowered the Erzton lord's war hammer to his side, and an answering knot of tension loosened in my own chest.

By this point, I had figured out most of the buttons and switches on the control panel, and I used them to shut down the psionic dampeners and other sensory-deprivation devices, disarm the traps, and open the maze exits. I also gave Jeffrey another vicious kick in the ribs, but he was still out cold, so I grabbed my trident and left the control room.

I should have gone slowly, just in case any more Hammers were lurking in the facility, but my steps quickened, and within seconds, I was running through the corridors. I raced down the stairs to the ground level and plunged into the maze.

Without the psionic dampeners, I was able to sense exactly

where Kyrion was, and it didn't take me long to reach the forest biodome. He was sitting on the bench watching the leaves twirl up and down in the man-made breeze. Roderick's hammer was now laid out across Kyrion's lap, like he didn't have the strength to hold it any longer, and the lunarium was barely glowing with his dark blue magic.

Tiredness rippled through the bond in continuous waves, along with the discomfort of the gruesome blaster burn on his left hand. The psionic shield Kyrion had used to wall off the injury was slowly cracking, allowing more pain to seep back into the Arrow's body and reverberate along the bond to me.

"Kyr!" I rushed forward. "Are you okay?"

It was a silly thing to ask, since I could feel just how much he was hurting, but Kyrion smiled at me anyway, and it was as warm and welcome as the sun breaking through a dark, stormy cloud.

He set the hammer aside and slowly hoisted himself onto his feet. He smiled at me again, but his shoulders slumped, and the sticky cobweb of him ached. "More or less. You?"

"More or less."

I put the trident down, and Kyrion stepped forward and cupped my cheek in his uninjured right hand. I stood on my tiptoes and pressed my lips to his. The air in the biodome was chilly, but Kyrion's lips were warm and firm, and I drank in the solid, quiet strength radiating off him.

Kyrion's hand drifted up into my hair, and he wound his fingers through the tangled locks and drew me closer. I curled my hands into his ruined jacket, relishing the steady beat of his heart underneath my fingertips. I drew in a breath, and his spearmint scent sank deep into my lungs, sharp and sweet, just like the blue-moon peonies in my mindscape.

The sticky cobweb of Kyrion in my mind vibrated with pleasure and relief. I hummed in response and deepened the kiss, my tongue flicking against his—

"I told you they were fine," a familiar voice said.

Kyrion and I broke apart.

Siya was now standing in the forest biodome. She lifted her war hammer and propped the weapon on her right shoulder, then jerked her chin at Kyrion and me. "They're well enough to kissy-kiss, so I'm assuming neither one of them is particularly close to dying."

Asterin stepped into the biodome, still clutching her silver blaster. She glanced back and forth between Kyrion and me, then sighed with relief.

"Any more Hammers in the facility?" I asked.

Siya shook her head. "No more Hammers are roaming around, and no guards are stationed outside. Looks like Roderick kept his inner circle pretty small. Not surprising, considering the circumstances."

Asterin walked over and stared down at Roderick. Her face paled, and her eyes darkened with grief. Thanks to Kyrion's telempathy, I could feel exactly how much she was hurting. The bumps and bruises the Hammers had given her were small stings compared with the spears of shock that kept lancing through her chest.

"I can't believe Roderick did this to us, to *me*. I thought he was . . ." Asterin's voice trailed off, and she shook her head in a violent motion, making her long black hair whip around her shoulders. "I don't know *what* I thought he was."

Siya stretched out a hand to comfort her stepsister, but Asterin skirted away. She didn't even see Siya's hand or the concern that creased the other woman's face.

A bitter laugh spewed out of Asterin's lips, and Siya, Kyrion, and I all grimaced at the harsh, caustic sound. "Yet again, I was completely wrong about someone," Asterin muttered. "Sometimes I think that's the story of my life."

The shock on her face quickly vanished, replaced by a disgusted sneer, although I couldn't tell if she was angrier at

Roderick for his horrid crimes or at herself for not seeing the charming lord for the cruel beast he had truly been.

Asterin sneered at Roderick's body a moment longer, then spun around and stalked away. Siya watched her leave, but she didn't call out to her stepsister.

In the distance, shouts sounded, along with a high, piercing whistle. Kyrion and I both tensed, but Siya waved her hand.

"That's Rigel giving me an all clear," she said. "I used my tablet to send him a distress call, but he was already on his way here, thanks to you, Vesper. I should go find him and the other House Collier Hammers. And Asterin too."

Siya nodded at us, then left the biodome.

Kyrion looked down at Roderick's body, and the sticky cobweb of him pulsed with even more weariness, along with an icy rage that took my breath away. "If I could, I would kill that bastard all over again for everything he's done," Kyrion growled. "To me, you, Asterin, Siya, and all the people he hunted and murdered in here."

I laid my hand on his upper right arm, careful of his injuries. "I know. Me too."

At my touch, Kyrion shuddered, and some of the icy rage thawed in his body. When he looked at me again, his eyes were calm, although his body sagged with exhaustion.

"Let's get out of here," Kyrion muttered. "I never want to see this place again."

I slipped my arm around his waist. Kyrion leaned on me, and together we left Roderick's body behind to be covered up by the swirling, falling leaves.

We returned to the control room to find Siya and Asterin talking to a man in his fifties with light brown hair and ruddy skin. The man was wearing the emerald green of House Collier, and his jacket stretched across his broad shoulders and stocky chest. Even though the battle was over and our enemies were dead, the lunarium hammer clenched in his fist was burning with a bright golden light.

Rigel's dark brown eyes flicked over Kyrion and me. No emotion showed on the other warrior's face, but the angry glare on his hammer dimmed in what I could have sworn was relief.

"I thought the two of you were going to do some simple training," Rigel rumbled. "Not dig up a scandal big enough to bring down a major House."

Kyrion shrugged. "Vesper and I are overachievers that way."

Rigel barked out a laugh and clapped Kyrion on the back, making the Arrow wince and wobble on his feet.

Rigel and the other House Collier Hammers quickly took control of the scene. First, they made sure all the House Battis warriors were dead and then gathered up their tablets and weapons. Rigel also sent some Hammers to the garage to see if any more explosives were attached to Siya's transport.

Meanwhile, Kyrion and I followed Siya and Asterin into the locker room. Siya opened the locker, and Kyrion and I fished out our stormswords, blasters, and tablets.

Kyrion plucked a skinbond injector off his silver bandolier of supplies and stabbed it into his upper left arm. The healing chemicals flooded his system, and some of the tense lines of pain eased in his face. He slowly curled his left fingers into a fist and opened them again, although the gruesome black blaster burn remained on his palm.

"You want to go into the infirmary and get healed by a medtable?" Siya asked.

Kyrion shook his head. "No. The medtable will make a record of my injuries, and the less House Battis knows about what happened, the safer we will all be. I can wait until we get back to the Collier estate."

Kyrion used a second skinbond injector on himself. He offered the other ones on his bandolier to me, Siya, and Asterin, but the three of us had minor injuries that didn't need immediate attention. None of us was in the best shape of our lives, but we would live.

The four of us returned to the control room. Jeffrey was still unconscious on the floor, but Siya cracked her hand across his jaw several times, and he finally jerked awake.

Jeffrey blinked and blinked, as if he didn't know where he was or what was going on. Slowly, his eyes sharpened, and he glanced from me to Kyrion to Siya to Asterin. The technician jerked back again, but he was trapped against the control panel, and there was nowhere for him to go.

"Listen closely, Jeffrey," Siya said in a deceptively light, pleasant voice. "You have two options. You can keep quiet and allow me the pleasure of breaking all the bones in your body with my hammer, or you can start talking and hope that I only leave you to rot in a House Collier detention facility. Your choice."

Jeffrey sucked in a breath. "It wasn't my idea. *None* of it was my idea. Roderick was behind it all, I swear! *He's* the one who lured people into the maze, not me . . ."

Jeffrey spilled his proverbial guts like the spineless coward he was. According to the technician, Roderick had been using the maze as his own personal playground for the last three years, and he'd lured dozens of people to the facility, locked them in the maze, and hunted them after hours.

"We used the lava to incinerate most of the bodies, but Roderick ordered the Hammers to bury a few of them," Jeffrey said. "In the flower beds in the garden biodome with the House Battis castle statues."

Disgust crinkled Kyrion's face. "So that's why some of the flowers in there were so much larger and more colorful than the others."

Siya shook her head. "More trophies," she muttered.

Asterin shuddered, her face pale and tight. Siya shot her a sympathetic look, but Asterin was too distraught to notice it.

I looked at Siya and raised my eyebrows in a silent question, and she shook her head again. Siya might have told me about Roderick cheating on Asterin all those years ago, but she wasn't going to reveal the information to her stepsister. At least, not tonight. That was probably for the best. Asterin didn't need any more heartbreak right now.

By the time Jeffrey finished talking, Rigel and the other House Collier Hammers had completed their sweep of the training facility.

Rigel stepped back into the control room. "We're clear. No other personnel are on-site."

Kyrion stabbed his finger toward the corridor. The bodies of the House Battis Hammers I'd killed were still sprawled across the floor. "What are you going to do with them?"

Siya swiped through a few screens on her tablet. "No idea. Right now, Aldrich and Verona think the best course of action is for us to quietly slip out of the facility, but I don't see how we're going to explain what happened to Roderick and his people. We can always claim they were alive when we left, but I doubt anyone will believe that." She sighed. "Either way, the story about Roderick's death will be all over the gossipcasts by morning."

"Is that a bad thing?" I asked.

Siya looked up from her tablet. "House Battis is arguably the most powerful of the Erzton Houses. They've never been particularly friendly to House Collier, but this will officially make them our enemies."

Kyrion frowned. "Even though you have footage of the Black Scarab and Roderick attacking Vesper and me in the maze?"

Siya shrugged. "We'll keep a copy of the footage, but I doubt it will be much help. Even if we release it to the gossipcasts,

Lady Battis will probably claim it's fake and that her darling son would *never* do anything so horrific. She'll do her best to discredit and undercut House Collier at every turn. Even if this incident doesn't boil up into an all-out war, Lady Battis still has enough money, influence, alliances, and resources to make life very, very difficult for us."

Rigel nodded, agreeing with Siya's assessment. Asterin's face paled again, and she clutched her stomach like she was going to be sick. Kyrion's forehead crinkled with concern.

"Then give everyone a different story to tell," I said, breaking the tense silence.

Rigel frowned. "What do you mean?"

I gestured over at the black box of explosives sitting on a nearby table. One of the House Collier warriors had retrieved it from the corridor and brought it into the control room. I also pulled the detonator out of my pocket and showed it to my friends. "Roderick was planning to blow up Siya's transport to explain away our deaths. I say we use his own trick against him."

Siya and Rigel exchanged a look. Asterin chewed on a fingernail and glanced back and forth between them.

"Roderick and his people dying in a transport crash *would* be a much more palatable story," Siya said. "The unexpected and tragic death of an heir to a major House."

Rigel tilted his head in agreement. "And no one in House Battis could point a finger back at House Collier and claim we were responsible for either the crash or Roderick's death."

The two of them stared at each other a moment longer, then both nodded. Asterin let out a soft sigh of relief.

Kyrion nudged me with his elbow. "Have I told you lately how brilliant you are, seer?"

I nudged him back with my own elbow. "You can never say it too often, Arrow."

He laughed, but then his eyes narrowed. "Why do I get the sense that smile on your face isn't just for me?"

"You're right. It's not just for you." I rubbed my hands together in glee. "I'm smiling because I'm finally going to get to blow some shit up."

Siya forced Jeffrey to download the footage of our battles in the maze onto our tablets, along with all the information he could access from the House Battis servers. Next, she made the technician erase all traces of us from the training facility, like the main control panel had malfunctioned and accidentally deleted all the surveillance from the last few hours.

Rigel and the other House Collier Hammers quickly cleaned up the blood and erased all the physical signs of a fight on the control level. Then they took the bodies, including Roderick's, down to the garage and loaded them onto the large House Battis transport I'd seen earlier.

Two hours later, it was like we had never been here at all.

I planted the black box of explosives on the ship and made sure the detonator I'd confiscated earlier was still working. I also engaged the transport's autopilot and synced it to Siya's ship so she could control both vehicles at once.

Once that was done, the Hammers loaded Jeffrey onto their ship, along with the lifeless Black Scarab from the maze, and headed for the Collier estate. Siya and Rigel wanted to blow the machine up along with the House Battis transport, but I'd convinced them to spare it. Studying the Scarab might tell us where it had come from, or more importantly, who had given it to Roderick and Jeffrey.

When everything was set, I boarded Siya's ship. She was at the controls, along with Rigel. Kyrion and Asterin were standing behind them. I joined my friends on the flight deck, and we left the transport garage.

Lucky for us, the training facility was located at the top of a rocky ridge, so no other businesses or homes were nearby. Siya steered her transport away from the facility, then set it in hover mode. She flipped some switches, took control of Roderick's ship, and also steered it out of the garage.

Siya maneuvered Roderick's ship so that it was drifting over a wide, deep chasm on this side of the mountain. "You're sure this will work?" she asked.

"Of course it will work." I waggled the black detonator at her. "I blew things up all the time in the R&D lab at Quill Corp."

"I didn't realize brewmakers needed to be tested in an explosive capacity," Rigel replied in a wry tone.

I grinned. "Well . . . they don't. At least, not so many times. But it was an excuse for me, Bodie, and the other lab rats to have a little fun. Explosion day was always the *best* day in the lab."

Siya and Rigel exchanged a look like they thought I was a few solar batteries short of a full charge. Kyrion let out a soft laugh at my dark humor, but Asterin stared dully at nothing, just as she had been doing ever since we left the control room.

I waggled the detonator at Siya and Rigel again. "You sure you want to do this? Destroy the evidence instead of revealing Roderick's crimes?"

Siya and Rigel exchanged another look, and they both nodded.

"We're sure," Siya replied in a firm voice. "House Collier can't afford to make an enemy of House Battis. Especially not now, when we're still recovering from the attack by the Serpens Corp mercenaries."

"Roderick should be punished for his crimes," Asterin muttered. It was the first time she had spoken in several minutes. "They should *all* be punished. They shouldn't just get away with it."

Siya hesitated. "Roderick and the others have been punished," she replied in a gentle tone. "They're dead, and we're not."

"What about all the people Roderick killed?" Asterin asked in a low, tense voice.

"Jeffrey gave us a list," Rigel chimed in. "He kept records of everyone Roderick lured into the maze just in case Roderick ever turned on him. We'll figure out a way to quietly notify the victims' families and tell them what happened. I don't know what else we can do, especially since Roderick and his people destroyed most of the bodies."

Asterin reluctantly nodded, but she didn't look at Siya or Rigel.

I know what I'll do, Asterin's voice muttered in my mind. *I'll leak the story to the gossipcasts as soon as House Collier is free of suspicion.*

Siya and Rigel didn't react, as though they hadn't heard Asterin's thought. I glanced at Kyrion, who shrugged. He'd also heard Asterin's vow, but he wasn't planning to do anything about it. Neither was I. Roderick should be held accountable for his horrific crimes, even in death.

Kyrion gestured out the window at Roderick's transport, which was still drifting over the chasm. "Won't the House Battis technicians comb through the wreckage to figure out what really happened?"

Siya shrugged. "Let them. Thanks to Jeffrey, there's no footage that we did anything wrong, and Roderick's explosives can only be traced back to him, not to House Collier. Our story is simple. You and Vesper trained in the maze, and then we all returned to House Collier. Roderick and his people left sometime later, their ship malfunctioned, and they were killed in the explosion."

"And what if Lady Battis realizes there's a body missing and that Jeffrey wasn't on board?" Asterin asked.

This time, Rigel shrugged. "Given the amount of explosives on the transport, it's going to be hard for anyone to find any remains in the wreckage. Besides, the techs will be focused on recovering Roderick's body. I doubt they'll search too hard for Jeffrey or anyone else."

It wasn't the neatest or cleanest cover story, but Siya and Rigel were right. With no security footage and decimated wreckage, it would be difficult, if not impossible, for Lady Battis to find any evidence, point a finger, and accuse us of any wrongdoing.

"Okay, last chance to change your minds," I warned my friends.

Siya and Rigel glanced at each other, then nodded. Asterin also nodded, although she still didn't look at anyone.

"Do it," Siya said.

I flipped the red switch.

BOOM!

The transport exploded in a massive fireball that lit up the night sky like a miniature sun. For a moment, the ship hovered in the air, burning brightly. Then it began to fall like a meteor dropping through the atmosphere . . .

BOOM!

The transport slammed into the bottom of the chasm. Another, larger fireball erupted, and within seconds, the entire ship was engulfed in flames.

Asterin spun around on her heel and left the flight deck. I wouldn't have wanted to watch the ship burn either. It was hard to realize that someone you had cared about, someone you had trusted with your heart and body, wasn't the person you thought. I'd experienced that same pain when I realized that Conrad Fawley had not only cheated on me but also agreed to help Rowena and Sabine Kent get rid of me.

"You should go check on Asterin," Rigel said.

He looked at Siya, who chewed on her lower lip. After a few seconds, she shook her head. "No, Asterin will think I'm gloating and saying *I told you so* about Roderick. You should do it."

Rigel nodded, then got up out of the copilot's seat and headed after Asterin.

Siya took hold of the controls and steered her ship away from the chasm. I kept staring through the windows. Maybe it was a quirk of my seer magic, but I could have sworn I saw Roderick's bloodred armor burning in the heart of the fire. I shivered.

Kyrion threaded his fingers through mine. "It's over. He can't hurt us anymore."

I squeezed his hand and leaned my head against his shoulder, drinking in the comforting warmth of his presence. Kyrion was right. Roderick Battis was dead, and he would never hunt—or kill—anyone else in his maze.

But I couldn't quite ignore my seer magic, which kept whispering that this wasn't the end of our problems—and that Roderick wasn't the only enemy who'd been behind this latest attack.

EIGHTEEN

KYRION

Siya's transport soared across the chasm and over the neighboring mountains, and we quickly returned to the Collier estate.

Rigel insisted we all go to the main infirmary and get checked out by the House Collier medics. Vesper, Asterin, and Siya were given some mild skinbonds, while I lay down on a medtable. Robotic needles pumped me full of more skinbonds, along with antibiotics and other medicines, then sloughed off and repaired the burned skin on both my left hand and my right forearm.

I stared up at Vesper through the clear polyplastic that covered the medtable. "You just like seeing me trapped in this bloody bubble," I groused.

Vesper grinned, leaned down, and tapped her finger on the plastic. "Yes, I do, especially when it's for your own good. Now, quit complaining and let the table finish its work."

I grumbled, but I couldn't hide my smile. After being on my own for so long, Vesper's fussing pleased and soothed my inner monster, who let out a little purr of satisfaction.

After I was healed and the medtable released me, Vesper and I joined Siya, Rigel, and Asterin in Lord Aldrich's library. Our friends had already told Aldrich and Verona everything that had happened, but Vesper and I chimed in and added our own stories to the mix.

The Erzton lord paced back and forth behind his desk, swiping through screens on his tablet. Aldrich had the same hazel eyes, straight nose, and light brown skin as Siya, although his hair was more iron-gray than black, given he was in his sixties. Verona stood off to the side, her hands clasped in front of her. The Erzton lady was a few years younger than her husband, and her long black hair and pale skin made her look like an older version of Asterin.

Verona's blue eyes flicked from her husband over to Vesper and me. I met her gaze and nodded. Verona gave me a grim smile and nodded back.

Aldrich tossed his tablet down onto his desk in disgust. "Roderick was luring people into his training facility and hunting them like animals?" He shook his head. "I still can't believe it."

"Believe it," I said in a wry voice, flexing my left fingers.

Despite the medtable's ministrations, my hand still ached, and I knew that I would feel the phantom sting of the lava-rigged blaster bolt for a long time, just as I would hear the echoes of Roderick's singsong voice as he stalked me through the maze.

Siya swiped through some screens on her own tablet. "According to the information Jeffrey gave us, Roderick killed more than four dozen people in the maze. No one ever traced any of the disappearances back to the training facility, and Roderick could have easily gone on hunting people for years to come."

"If he hadn't decided to pick Kyrion and Vesper as his next targets," Verona said in a soft voice.

Vesper crossed her arms over her chest. "And that's my main question. *Why* would he do that?"

Everyone looked at her.

"What do you mean?" Siya asked.

Vesper gestured back and forth between herself and me. "Why would Roderick pick Kyrion and me as his next targets? Why *us* specifically and not some other truebonded couple?"

"Roderick told Kyrion he wanted a challenge," Rigel replied. "That he wanted to test his skills against the best of the best."

Vesper nodded. "Maybe he did. But if Roderick truly wanted to test his skills, then why not take us *both* on at once?"

"Because deep down, he was a fucking coward who didn't want to risk losing," Asterin chimed in, her voice dripping with venom.

She hadn't said much since Vesper and I had entered the library. Everyone stared at her now, but Asterin crossed her arms over her chest and kept her gaze fixed on the flames crackling in the fireplace.

Vesper cleared her throat, breaking the awkward silence. "Plus, the Black Scarab in the maze was trying to capture me, not kill me. Then, later on, in the control room when Jeffrey realized I wasn't in the maze anymore, he also told the House Battis Hammers to capture me, not kill me. Jeffrey didn't want to ruin some deal Roderick had made."

Aldrich frowned. "You think something else was going on? That there was some other reason Roderick lured you both into the maze?"

Vesper nodded. "I think it's a strong possibility."

"Like what?" Verona asked.

Vesper shrugged. "I'm not sure. Roderick might have wanted Kyrion and me in the maze, but he also wanted us separated. He also wanted to kill Kyrion but not me."

Her lips puckered, and her gaze grew distant, as though she was considering a hundred possibilities to explain Roderick's odd actions. The velvety ribbon of her also hummed in my mind.

Anything you want to share? I asked.

Vesper shook her head the tiniest bit. *It's just a theory. I need to think about it some more. I don't want to tell the others unless I'm absolutely certain.*

"Well, I don't care about Roderick Battis's motives, only his actions." Aldrich shot another disgusted look at the tablet still lying on his desk.

"What do you want to do?" Verona asked in a soft voice.

Aldrich started pacing again. "That's the problem. I can't *do* much of anything. I can't approach anyone at House Battis with this information. If they didn't know what Roderick was doing, they'll be stunned. Most likely, they won't believe me."

"And if they did know what Roderick was doing?" Asterin muttered, still staring into the crackling flames in the fireplace.

"Then they'll deny it and cover up the scandal even more so than they already have." Aldrich stopped pacing, then scooped up his tablet. "Either way, news of the transport crash has already hit the gossipcasts, so I need to follow protocol, reach out to Lady Battis, and offer my condolences for her loss."

I studied the Erzton lord. "*Protocol?* That's a nice way of saying you're going to see how Lady Battis reacts. That will tell you everything you need to know about what she and the other leaders of House Battis really knew about Roderick and the training facility."

A sly smile curved Aldrich's lips. "Something like that."

Admiration filled me. The Erzton lord played noble games as well as anyone I'd ever met. Even with Jeffrey in House Collier custody, it was smart—and devious—of Lord Aldrich to use a condolence call to slyly gather more information.

Verona, Siya, and Rigel nodded, but more disgust twisted Asterin's face. She spun away from the fireplace, wrenched a door open, and left the library.

"I'll go check on her," Verona murmured.

"No," I said. "Let me."

The lady glanced at me in surprise, but she nodded.

I touched Vesper's elbow. "I'll meet you back in our suite."

Vesper also nodded, and I left the library.

I found Asterin on a walkway that connected the main castle to the guest wing. Her elbows were resting on the railing, and she was slumped forward, like the stone was the only thing holding her upright. I stepped up beside Asterin and mimicked her stance.

The earlier snow had moved out, and above us, the Frozon moon was shining brightly in the night sky, along with a smattering of stars. The silvery moon- and starlight streamed in through the clear energy shield that covered the estate and gilded the petals of the blue-moon peonies in the large topiary garden at the heart of the grounds.

"Did my mother send you to check on me?" Asterin muttered.

"No, I volunteered."

She huffed. "Why? Did Siya not want to come and brag about how she'd been right about Roderick all along?"

"Once upon a time, I was involved with a woman named Francesca," I said, changing the subject. "She was wonderful. Smart, witty, fun, beautiful. I thought I had finally found a bit of happiness after years of just surviving and going through the motions of life after my parents' deaths."

Asterin eyed me warily. "What happened?"

"I found a bottle of perfume in Francesca's things. Only it wasn't perfume—it was a chembond."

Unlike skinbonds, which were designed to heal cut skin, broken bones, and the like, chembonds were used to connect two people for a short period of time. Chembonds had a variety of academic and military uses, but they were mainly used as aphrodisiacs, especially at nightclubs and other places where people were looking to feel a little less lonely, if only for a few hours.

Asterin blanched. "She was dosing you with a chembond to make you fall for her?"

I nodded. A knot of emotion clogged my throat, and my inner monster snarled. Even after all these years, cold rage still flooded my veins like an ocean of ice every time I thought about how Francesca had fooled me.

Asterin winced. "I'm so sorry, Kyrion. That must have been awful."

I cleared my throat. "It was awful. What Francesca did was horrible, of course, but to me, the worst part was how *stupid* I felt afterward. For not realizing what she was really doing and that she cared much more about the Caldaren fortune than she ever did about me."

Sympathy creased Asterin's face, and some of the tension trickled out of her body. She let out a weary sigh and stared out over the garden again. "When the House Battis Hammers attacked me and Siya in the control room, I thought it was a giant misunderstanding. Or that Jeffrey was the one giving the orders. But then Jeffrey started talking to Roderick in the maze, and I realized Roderick was in charge and that he was going to kill me and Siya and you and Vesper just because he wanted to—just for *a bit of sport*, as he called it."

Asterin shook her head, tears gleaming in her eyes. "How could I have been so *wrong* about him?"

"It's easy to be wrong about people. Especially people like Francesca and Roderick who only show you what they want you to see and nothing of their true selves. You didn't do anything wrong."

Asterin barked out a harsh laugh. "It feels like I did *everything* wrong, at least when it came to Roderick."

"It's not wrong to believe in people. Someday someone will come along who will deserve your trust, who will *earn* it," I replied in a serious voice. "Don't let the Francescas and the Rodericks of the galaxy take that possibility away from you. Because that's when they truly win."

Asterin gave me a smile, but the thin, wan expression didn't reach her eyes, and hurt rippled off her and twinged my telempathy. She turned and stared back out over the garden again. I didn't say anything else. I just stood there with her until the moon finally disappeared behind some clouds.

Eventually, Asterin muttered that she was tired and going inside, but she made no move to actually leave the walkway. I bade her good night and left my friend to her brooding.

Words were all well and good, but it would take Asterin a while to recover from Roderick's betrayal. Not just his plan to kill us tonight but all the other ways and times he had betrayed her over the years without her even realizing it. Asterin would probably examine everything Roderick had ever said and done in a new light, just as I had when I'd realized Francesca was drugging me.

I stepped into the guest wing and made my way to the luxurious suite I was sharing with Vesper. She was standing by a table, swiping through the files Jeffrey had given Siya and Rigel. A couple of gossipcast feeds also flickered over the table, showing footage of Roderick's transport burning at the bottom of the chasm.

"How is Asterin?" Vesper asked.

I shrugged. "I hope I left her a little better than before, but it's hard to tell. Asterin doesn't wear her heart on her sleeve."

Vesper arched an eyebrow. "Sounds like someone else I know."

I snorted and then wished I hadn't, since the motion made my entire body ache. As much as I wanted to fall face-first on the floor and lie there for a week, I was a dirty, sweaty mess, so I headed into the bathroom to take a shower. Vesper followed me.

Despite being healed, I was still moving gingerly. So was Vesper, and together we helped each other out of our ruined clothes. I stuffed the garments into a recycler in the corner, and then Vesper held out her hand and drew me into the shower.

Like everything else at the Collier estate, the shower was the epitome of luxury, with jets that spewed water in all directions. I turned on the water and let it beat down on my back in a hard, warm spray. I quickly soaped up my hair and body, then let the soothing streams of water rinse away the dirt, grime, and blood of the maze. Vesper did the same thing.

When we were finished, we donned plush green robes and went into the bedroom. I lay down on the bed, and Vesper curled up beside me, resting her head on my chest. I wrapped my arm around her, and we lay there for a long time, just soaking up the quiet solace of each other's presence.

"I knew you were injured," Vesper said in a low voice. "I felt it through the bond. But I had no idea about the lava until I opened your door in my mindscape and astrally projected myself into the maze. Blasted lava." She snarled the last few words like they were a vile curse.

"Yes, we do have a rather bad and alarming habit of being around lava," I quipped. "We definitely need to work on that part of our bond."

Vesper laughed, then shivered against my body. "I came so close to losing you tonight, Kyr."

"You will *never* lose me," I vowed, tightening my grip on her.

Vesper snuggled closer and buried her face in my neck. Her warm breath tickled my skin, and my body responded to her the way it always did. Wanting, aching, yearning for more.

I smoothed my hand down her hair, which was still damp from the shower. Vesper raised her head, and we stared at each other. The silver flecks in her dark blue eyes were brighter and more luminous than stars in a midnight sky, and I could have happily spent the rest of my life studying how they flickered, flashed, and flared with her moods and emotions.

I dipped my head and brushed my lips against hers. Vesper

hummed with pleasure, cupped my face in her hands, and deepened the kiss.

The first touch of her tongue against mine was like a match igniting everything inside me, and my inner monster roared with hunger. I growled, embraced that hunger, and pulled Vesper even closer so that she was straddling me. Fire boiled up in my veins, and I was already hard and aching for her.

Vesper rocked against me, both of us wearing only our robes. Her slick heat brushed up against my dick, which stiffened that much more.

I groaned. "If you keep that up, this isn't going to last very long."

Vesper sat back and tugged the belt loose on my robe. She tossed one half of the garment aside, then the other, then let out a low whistle of appreciation. My dick stood at attention, and the heat of her gaze scorched me just as much as her touch did.

"Oh, I think I can make it last a good long while," Vesper purred.

She gave me a mischievous smile, then wiggled down and put her mouth on me.

I sucked in a breath, every muscle in my body clenching. My hips bucked up off the bed, and my hands fisted in the blankets.

Vesper worked me with her lips, tongue, and fingers. Fast, then slow. Soft, then hard. Each lick, suck, and caress made arrows of pleasure zing through my body, like I was a machine and every single part of me was being jolted back to life.

Nothing had ever felt so bloody *good*.

Those electric arrows merged together, coalescing into white-hot heat that was more intense than anything I'd experienced in the Magma biodome. My toes curled, stars flashed in my eyes, and I jerked against her hand, finding my release.

Vesper kept stroking me the whole time, and the velvety ribbon of her in my mind hummed with pleasure, matching the zing of electricity still sparking and crackling through my own body.

NINETEEN

VESPER

Kyrion finally relaxed, his eyes such a dark blue they looked almost black. His body sank into the bed, as though he was suddenly boneless, and the sticky cobweb of him in my mind reverberated with pleasure.

"I would say that lasted a good long while, wouldn't you, Kyr?" I said in a smug voice.

He blinked a few times. Some of the hot glaze faded from his eyes, and his gaze sharpened. In an instant, he was once again the arrogant Regal lord and dangerous Arrow I knew so well.

"That sounded distinctly like a challenge," Kyrion growled.

He sat up, bringing me with him. I laughed, and Kyrion pressed a quick kiss to my lips.

"Silence, now," he murmured. "I need to concentrate."

Kyrion loosened the belt on my robe and peeled the garment off my left shoulder, then my right shoulder. The second it slid down my back, he used his telekinesis to fling it aside, along with his own robe, so that there was nothing between us.

Kyrion raked his gaze over my body the same way I had

done to his. I shivered, and I could have sworn I could see the heat of my desire reflected in Kyrion's eyes, which had once again turned more black than blue. Or maybe that was just all our emotions mixing, mingling, and reverberating through the bond. Either way, it was one of the most dizzying, exhilarating sensations I'd ever experienced.

Kyrion leaned forward, nuzzling my neck. "I love the way my shampoo smells on your skin. Soft and sweet, just like you."

"And I love you," I replied, winding my arms around his neck.

Kyrion grabbed my hips, anchoring me to him, then flipped us over so that I was on my back. He braced his forearms on either side of my body, looming over me the way he always did. Even though he wasn't touching me, the heat of his body soaked into my own, and I shivered with anticipation.

"You had your turn, but I'm rather fond of this position," he declared.

I arched an eyebrow, then skimmed my fingers along his broad, strong shoulders, enjoying the bunch and flex of his muscles under my touch.

"Really? Why is that?" I asked, putting a teasing note in my voice.

Kyrion gave me a wicked grin, then dipped his head and nuzzled my neck again. He trailed light butterfly kisses down my chest, then drew my right nipple into his mouth and sucked on it hard. A spike of pleasure jolted through me.

My breath quickened, and I dragged my nails along his scalp. "There is something to be said for this position."

"Mm-hmm," Kyrion murmured again my skin.

He lavished attention on first one nipple, then the other, until I was squirming against him the same way he had been squirming against me earlier. Kyrion lifted his head, and I wound my arms around his neck and drew his mouth down to mine.

His lips and tongue were hot and heavy against my own,

and I tried to tug him down, wanting to feel his weight on top of me, but Kyrion braced himself on one forearm. His hand slid down my stomach, then between my thighs, and he rubbed his fingers against me, sending more spikes of pleasure shooting out through my body.

My back arched at the heady sensations, and Kyrion leaned down and licked at the rapid pulse beating in my throat even as he kept rubbing his fingers against me.

"I love the little purrs of pleasure you make," he rumbled against my skin. "And I love you too."

I was too mindless with desire to do anything but moan in response.

Kyrion kept teasing me with his fingers, and I ran my hands all over his body, trying to bring him the same amount of pleasure he was bringing me. We both had birth-control implants, so there was no awkward fumbling between us. Just one kiss, caress, and wave of pleasure after another.

I panted at the quick slide and glide of his fingers. "Kyr . . . Kyr . . ."

"Do you know what my favorite part about this position is?" he murmured.

I was once again too mindless to do anything but moan in response.

"This," Kyrion said.

He lifted my right leg, then slowly slid inside me. I gasped again and dug my fingers into his shoulders. Kyrion's mouth landed on mine, and he devoured me the same way I was devouring him. He kissed me again and again, timing his thrusts to the flick of his tongue against my lips.

I lifted my other leg and locked it around his waist. Kyrion growled and slid even deeper inside me. We were both panting now, rocking together fast and furiously.

This was no distant dream. This was him and me. Now. Here. Together.

And it was the most glorious thing in the galaxy.

Afterward, we lay on the bed, arms and legs tangled, the afterglow bouncing from me to Kyrion and back again through the bond.

"I could stay like this forever," he declared.

I nuzzled his jaw with my nose. "Me too."

He turned onto his side and drew me into his arms so that we were face-to-face. I pushed a lock of black hair off his forehead. I loved seeing Kyrion like this, completely at ease and totally relaxed, and the same sensations reverberated through the bond. I would never forget the horrors we had faced in the maze, but right now I was going to enjoy every single second of our time together.

Kyrion ran his hands up and down my arms. Then he frowned, and the sticky cobweb in my mind pulsed with curiosity and more than a touch of wariness. "Did you find anything in Jeffrey's files to support your theory that someone else was involved with Roderick Battis?"

I shook my head. "Nothing yet, but I messaged Daichi and Tivona right before you returned to the suite."

Daichi Hirano was Kyrion's chief of staff. He was currently hiding out on Corios with his uncle, Touma Hirano, a spelltech who dabbled in all sorts of illegal things. Tivona Winslow was my best friend and a skilled negotiator who was running Quill Corp in my absence. The three of them, along with Zane, had been gathering intel and keeping an eye on things in the Imperium while Kyrion and I were on the run.

"Daichi and Tivona will help me with the files tomorrow," I continued. "I'm going to take a closer look at everything in the morning, but I'm pretty sure of what I'll find."

Kyrion's frown deepened. "Which is what, exactly?"

I explained my theory, and Kyrion's face darkened like a storm cloud.

"Are you sure?" he growled.

I considered his question. I wasn't sure. Not in a proven, scientific way like I would be when testing a new brewmaker or blaster in the R&D lab, but my seer magic kept whispering that I was right. "Yes, I'm sure."

Kyrion spat out a string of colorful curses. "I don't know who's worse, the Techwave or Callus Holloway."

"I would vote for Holloway. The Techwave just wants to use and kill me. Holloway wants us both under his thumb to drain and torture as long as possible."

Kyrion's eyes darkened again, and the sticky cobweb of him bristled with anger. I traced my fingers over his forehead, trying to smooth out the deep, worried line there. Kyrion sighed, then leaned into my touch.

"We need to deal with the Techwave and Holloway," he said. "Take the fight to them."

I nodded and kept tracing my fingers over his forehead. "I have some ideas about how we can do that—tomorrow."

I pushed on his shoulders so that he was lying flat on his back. "Our enemies can wait. Right now I am much more interested in you and me and making the most of this big, comfortable bed."

I slung my leg over his hips so that I was straddling him again. I rocked forward, and he hardened beneath me once more. The frown vanished from Kyrion's face, although his eyes quickly grew darker again, this time with desire.

I grinned. "There's another position I want to try. Care to guess what it is?"

Kyrion growled and pulled my head down to his. Our lips met, and everything else melted away. At least for the rest of this night.

EPILOGUE

NEREZZA

"At this time, investigators believe mechanical issues are to blame for the transport crash, which claimed the life of Roderick Battis, the presumed heir of House Battis, along with several other members of House Battis . . ."

General Orion Ocnus crossed his arms over his chest and shook his head. The overhead lights made his short dark brown hair look like needles jutting up out of his ruddy scalp. "Another bloody failure. This is becoming a bad habit of yours, Nerezza."

At his snide comment, my hand fisted around my wineglass. Fury roared through me, but I resisted the urge to hurl the glass at Ocnus. The general was standing next to me, and we were both in my luxurious suite, watching the gossipcast images of the transport crash on the holoscreen. I wasn't going to soil my own space by doing something so childish as throwing wine in the condescending bastard's face. No matter how much I wanted to.

Ocnus turned toward me, his bushy eyebrows lifting, like

he could sense my white-hot rage. Maybe he could. Despite my loathing of him, Ocnus was nothing if not observant. A clear challenge sparked in his black eyes, as though he was daring me to reveal my true feelings about the situation and especially him, but I wasn't going to fall into that trap.

I raised the glass to my lips and took a slow, deliberate sip. The wine was an excellent vintage, with notes of apples and berries, but right now it puckered my tongue like vinegar. I swallowed the wine and plastered a benign expression on my face.

An angry flush crept up Ocnus's neck. He didn't like being kept waiting. Too damn bad.

"If you'll recall, approaching Roderick Battis was *your* idea," I replied, my voice as smooth and even as the glass in my hand.

Ocnus harrumphed. "Yes, well, *you're* the one who made the arrangements."

Ocnus had come to me with his plan several days ago. He'd leveraged someone in House Battis into becoming his spy in the Erzton. Ocnus's spy had told the general about Roderick Battis's dome of death, and Ocnus had seen a chance to capture Vesper Quill.

Despite all the information I'd stolen from the Serpens Corp servers, the Techwave scientists still weren't any closer to figuring out how to fix Ocnus's new hand cannon, which was based on Vesper's design. So Ocnus still needed to get his hands on my long-lost daughter in order to mass-produce the Techwave's weapon.

All things considered, Ocnus's plan hadn't been a bad one. He'd told me to contact Roderick Battis with an offer: invite Vesper Quill and Kyrion Caldaren to his training facility, or face the consequences of the Techwave leaking the info about what he was really doing in his maze to the Erzton gossipcasts.

Blackmail was one of my favorite pastimes. Knowing which

buttons on a person's psyche to press and for how long and hard was an art form that I had mastered long ago. Roderick Battis had been exceedingly arrogant, and it had been highly amusing to watch him squirm. Roderick had done what people always did when they were cornered: deny he had done anything wrong, and then when confronted with the irrefutable evidence of his guilt, he'd tried to bribe me to look the other way.

In many ways, people were just like instruments, and all you had to do was figure out which strings to pluck to get them to do exactly what you wanted. My social-engineering ability let me see those internal strings, but Roderick had been easier to manipulate than most, and I'd played the Erzton lord like a maestro conducting an orchestra.

Roderick had fancied himself a hunter, so I'd given him a big-game prize in Kyrion Caldaren. Ocnus had even supplied Roderick with a Black Scarab and a new prototype armor the Techie scientists were trying to perfect for the human soldiers. Something else Vesper would have been able to help with, if only things had gone according to Ocnus's plan.

Ocnus kept staring at me, that accusatory look still on his face. I took another sip of my vinegary wine.

"I might have made the arrangements, but *you're* the one who supplied the weapons. Maybe you should have given Roderick more Scarabs to capture Vesper and help him kill Kyrion, instead of just a single machine and one suit of modified armor."

Ocnus waved his hand. "Bah! Even with the best armor credits could buy, a pampered lord like Roderick Battis would never have gotten the better of a battle-hardened warrior like Kyrion Caldaren. Roderick was just supposed to keep Kyrion busy and out of the way while the Scarab captured Vesper in the maze and the House Battis Hammers escorted her to our ship." His face darkened. "But things didn't go according to my plan."

"Funny how that seems to keep happening to you," I replied, my voice still velvety smooth.

Another angry flush swept up Ocnus's neck, and he glared at me for a moment before flapping his hand at the holoscreen. "Can anything be traced back to us?"

"Of course not," I lied. "I contacted Roderick through a secure private channel, and the Black Scarab and modified armor were sent to the House Battis training facility. There's no way Vesper, Kyrion, or anyone at House Collier will be able to trace anything back to us."

That wasn't entirely true, but Ocnus didn't need to know that. Oh, I had contacted Roderick through secure means, and the equipment had gone to his facility, but I had no idea who Roderick might have bragged to about what he was doing. It was entirely possible he had told someone his goal was to kill Kyrion and kidnap Vesper—and exactly who was funding his latest hunting expedition.

That part of the plan had been my idea. As amusing as it would have been to capture Kyrion and torture him for all the wrongs he'd done to me, Vesper was much more likely to be quickly, thoroughly broken if her truebonded partner was dead, so I'd told Roderick to make sure Vesper was captured, and then to kill Kyrion as quickly as possible.

But I was guessing the Erzton lord had ignored my orders and decided to hunt the dangerous Arrow instead of imme-diately eliminating him. Now Roderick was dead as a result of his own foolishness. Still, it was no great loss, especially since I got the delightful bonus of chiding Ocnus about his plan failing.

Ocnus watched the crash reporting on the holoscreen for a few more seconds, then stabbed his finger at me. "You have to fix this, Nerezza. We still need Vesper's expertise before we can mass-produce the hand cannon, and we could also use her brain on a few more projects." He shook his head. "You look so much like your daughter, yet you have none of her mechanical ingenuity. What a shame."

I ground my teeth and tipped my head at him. "Understood. I'll start working on a new approach."

Ocnus eyed me like he thought I was going to set my wine down and get started right away. The general didn't realize that he was just as expendable as Roderick Battis, and by the time he figured it out, it would be too late—for him, of course.

I took another sip of wine. Ocnus huffed again, then spun around on his heel, wrenched the door open, and stormed away.

"Good riddance," I muttered.

The crash footage kept playing on the screen. Ocnus's spy hadn't found out exactly what had happened yet, but I was willing to bet Vesper was behind everything that had gone wrong.

Roderick had messaged me when Vesper and Kyrion had arrived at his facility and then again when they had entered his maze. My plan to separate and isolate the couple had worked perfectly, but everything else had failed miserably. Somehow, Vesper and Kyrion had taken down Roderick, and then Vesper must have orchestrated the ship crash to hide the fact that she and Kyrion had killed the Erzton lord and his people. Every time I thought I had the perfect plan to finally take care of her once and for all, the girl squirmed away from me yet again.

More white-hot fury roared through me, and for once, I couldn't contain it. I spun away from the holoscreen and hurled the wineglass at a nearby window. The delicate glass shattered on impact, although the sturdy window itself remained intact. I stood there, breathing hard, my chest heaving, my entire body vibrating with fury. I wasn't quite sure why. This wasn't the first time my plans had been foiled, but Vesper and Kyrion were quite possibly the most formidable, frustrating enemies I had ever encountered.

I *despised* losing, especially to the same people over and over again.

I stood there watching the wine drip down the window for several seconds. Then I blew out a breath and calmed myself. I went over and hit a button on my desk. A voice crackled through the speaker embedded in the table. "Yes, ma'am?"

"Send a cleaning crew in here," I commanded. "I spilled some wine."

"Yes, ma'am," the voice replied. "Right away."

I yanked the chair out from behind the desk, sat down, and turned off the gossipcast. Then I used the holoscreen to start swiping through one file after another. Roderick Battis might have gotten himself killed, but he'd given me access to more Erzton secrets than he realized. All I had to do was find the right one, connected to the right person, and I would get everything I had ever wanted.

And then I would finally eliminate all my enemies, starting with General Orion Ocnus, then Callus Holloway and Kyrion Caldaren, and, finally, Vesper Quill.

Thank you for reading ***Only Rogue Actions***.
Vesper Quill and Kyrion Caldaren will return
in another **Galactic Bonds** adventure.

ABOUT THE AUTHOR

Jennifer Estep is a *New York Times*, *USA Today*, and internationally bestselling author who prowls the streets of her imagination in search of her next fantasy idea.

Jennifer is the author of the **Galactic Bonds**, **Section 47**, **Elemental Assassin**, **Crown of Shards**, **Gargoyle Queen**, and other fantasy series. She has written more than fifty books, along with numerous novellas and stories.

In her spare time, Jennifer enjoys hanging out with friends and family, doing yoga, and reading fantasy and romance books. She also watches way too much TV and loves all things related to superheroes.

For more information on Jennifer and her books, visit her website at www.jenniferestep.com or follow her online on Facebook, Instagram, Threads, Bluesky, Amazon, BookBub, Goodreads, TikTok, and X (formerly Twitter).

Happy reading, everyone!

To sign up for Jennifer's newsletter,
scan the QR code or visit
https://bit.ly/41AGJvn

OTHER BOOKS
BY JENNIFER ESTEP

THE GALACTIC BONDS SERIES
Only Bad Options
Only Good Enemies
Only Hard Problems (Zane Zimmer book)
Only Cold Depths
Only Rogue Actions

THE SECTION 47 SERIES
A Sense of Danger
Sugar Plum Spies (holiday book)
A Touch of Treachery

The Elemental Assassin series
FEATURING GIN BLANCO

BOOKS
Spider's Bite
Web of Lies
Venom
Tangled Threads
Spider's Revenge
By a Thread
Widow's Web
Deadly Sting
Heart of Venom
The Spider
Poison Promise

Black Widow
Spider's Trap
Bitter Bite
Unraveled
Snared
Venom in the Veins
Sharpest Sting
Last Strand
Stings and Stones (short story collection)

E-NOVELLAS AND SHORT STORIES
Haints and Hobwebs
Thread of Death
Parlor Tricks
Kiss of Venom
Unwanted
Nice Guys Bite
Winter's Web
Heart Stings
Spider and Frost (crossover novella)

THE CROWN OF SHARDS SERIES
Kill the Queen
Protect the Prince
Crush the King

THE GARGOYLE QUEEN SERIES
Capture the Crown
Tear Down the Throne
Conquer the Kingdom

THE BLACK BLADE SERIES
Cold Burn of Magic
Dark Heart of Magic
Bright Blaze of Magic

THE BIGTIME SERIES
Karma Girl
Hot Mama
Jinx
A Karma Girl Christmas (holiday novella)
Nightingale
Fandemic

THE MYTHOS ACADEMY SPINOFF SERIES
FEATURING RORY FORSETI

Spartan Heart
Spartan Promise
Spartan Destiny

THE MYTHOS ACADEMY SERIES
FEATURING GWEN FROST

BOOKS
Touch of Frost
Kiss of Frost
Dark Frost
Crimson Frost
Midnight Frost
Killer Frost

E-NOVELLAS AND SHORT STORIES
First Frost
Halloween Frost
Spartan Frost
Spider and Frost (crossover novella)

OTHER WORKS
The Beauty of Being a Beast (fairy tale)
Write Your Own Cake: A Worldbuilding Essay
Write Your Own Cake: Tips for Writing a Long Series